Opaline's
The Witch DNA #1
Discovery

SONJA GUNTER

one

"Welcome to Speed Dating Night at Holiday Inn. I'm the new event director, Opaline Lunn. May I have your name?" The gorgeous woman standing in front of her had a beautiful oval face, framed with wayward auburn hair. *Why would someone who looked like her need to be dating?* Opaline wondered as she waited for the woman to speak.

"Hi—yeah—I'm Ebba. Ebba Mignon."

"Is this your first time at a speed dating event?"

"No, I've attended several. Still looking for Mr. Right." Ebba laughed.

Opaline smiled. "You might find him. I have about fifty people scheduled to participate tonight."

"Really? Oh my." Ebba fluffed her hair. "I didn't know we had that many single people in Onamia."

"I thought the same thing last night when I checked all the confirmations. Here is your packet with your name tag."

"Thank you."

Opaline casually watched Ebba walk into the banquet room. Mulling over the comment of how many people would be in attendance, she pressed her lips together. It had been odd. When she had checked Facebook after making a cup of tea, the confirmed attendees list had gone from zero to thirty in five minutes. Thinking she had done something wrong, she had double-checked the event she'd posted on Facebook. She had the right day, Wednesday. Nothing pointed to an error on her part.

What a newbie she had been. Her lack of knowledge of speed dating had worked against her, it seemed. With Onamia being a small city in Minnesota, and with just over eight hundred and fifty permanent residents in a given year, Ebba was correct. Fifty was an unusually large number of singles for her small town. The only thing Opaline could come up with was that her post had encouraged the residents of Mille Lacs Lake, which is only a few miles away, to sign up.

But that theory had blown up on her too. The confirmed-attendees file had shown that people were coming from as far as Little Falls, which was a good half hour drive away.

Per Mr. Horton's email, the owner of the speed dating franchise, the norm for an event was twenty people. That number had risen to forty-seven in minutes. *No,* she corrected, *forty-eight, including herself.*

It was a sold-out event.

She shouldn't be complaining. It was definitely a plus. All forty-seven attendees had confirmed and paid thirty dollars via PayPal or Apple Pay.

Which was awesome.

As she tallied the numbers, she realized it meant her

first paycheck of seventy-five percent commission would be more than she had presumed. It was much needed in her current financial situation.

From a distance, she saw another woman coming and waited for her to approach the table. "Hello, welcome to Speed Dating Night at Holiday Inn. I'm your host for this evening's event, Opaline Lunn. May I have your name?"

Before she was able to finish with her, more men and women arrived. Someone, or something, was telling her things were changing in her life.

Taking a deep breath, Opaline concentrated on giving each of the attendees her undivided attention. She knew the importance of receiving good reviews.

Soon the line trickled down, and three-fourths of the attendees had checked in. She took a sip of water, glanced up, and noticed a man with black hair near the end of the line. He smiled and laughed at something the woman in front of him said. Even from this distance, she saw how it had made his blue eyes sparkle in the lights.

Holy smokes! He was a looker. Why would he be here? He had to have a girlfriend.

"Will you be speed dating tonight? I'm Scott."

Opaline blinked to focus on the man in front of her and not the one farther down the line. She looked at the check-in list for the man's first name. "Sorry, Scott. Can I have your last name too?"

"Sure, Morre. Scott Morre."

"Thank you. I found you. And again, I'm sorry. What was the question you asked?" She set down the pen and looked at Scott, giving him her full attention.

"I was wondering, Opaline, if you were going to be participating in the event tonight."

She tried not to recoil at the way he had said her name. The way he had emphasized the last part of it had a creepy sexual vibration to it. Opaline swallowed hard. "I am. I look forward to our date."

"So will I." Scott grinned, showing off perfectly aligned white teeth.

She clamped her lips together, not trusting herself to say anything more, and gave him a packet. He took the papers, turned, and winked at the woman behind him in line.

I don't think so, she thought.

She put a big fat *N* next to his name. Scott was *not* someone she wanted to date. The man was clearly a player.

Lifting her head, she forced a smile as the woman Scott had winked at took his place in line to stand in front of Opaline. "Hello, I'm Opaline."

"Hi. I'm Paula Dayan, and this is my big brother, Eamon."

"Welcome to Speed Dating Night. We have a full house." Opaline marked off their names and then held out two packets.

Paula's brother moved from behind her, and Opaline realized he was the man with black hair that she had noticed earlier.

"This is Eamon's first time, but I've been to a couple of the events before. And oh, I'm so glad you narrowed down the age group. I was getting tired of old men asking me out," Paula stated as she took one of the packets.

"I'm sorry that happened. I'm the new consultant for this area. The old one recently got married."

She laughed, and Paula joined in at the corny joke.

However, Eamon only smiled a little. The spark she had noticed earlier didn't reach his eyes this time.

"Eamon, I'm sorry you didn't find my play on words funny. In your packet, you will find a suggested list of questions to ask your dates. If you should find some of the ladies compatible, you will have the opportunity to stay for our second session."

Still holding his packet, she set it down and tapped it with her finger, feeling strangely lightheaded. He moved to stand in front of her, forcing her to look at him. In doing so, she couldn't miss how toned and buff his body was from the waist up. His T-shirt only emphasized what it hid.

"Let me get this straight. If I think I might like to have a real date with someone, I should ask them to stay?"

"Yes and no. In here." Opaline paused to catch her breath. She blinked and then pushed the file toward him. "This a list of everyone who has signed up for tonight. While dating during the first session, simply put a mark by their name. If those parties are interested in another session, you will be able to speed date again."

"Oh, Eamon, it's no wonder you don't have a girl-friend. I'm sorry, Opaline. I'll make sure he gets the hang of this. I'm very confident my big bro will find someone tonight." Paula took his packet too.

"Enjoy your dates."

"Thank you, Opaline. Will you be speed dating tonight also?"

"I will."

"Come on, Eamon. There is a line behind us. Let's go get a drink." Paula tugged on her brother's arm.

Opaline watched Eamon's mouth curve upward. The

smile, this time, did make his eyes sparkle. As he walked away, she felt a weird sense of loneliness. His presence had given her a familiar feeling. She wanted to follow and be close to him.

Frowning at her odd thought, she shook her head to clear her mind and then greeted the next participant. Thankfully, she noted the line had thinned down, and there were only a few more people to check in before the start time at seven.

Opaline sat for a moment at the table, waiting for the last two people to arrive. Even if they didn't, forty-five attendees wasn't bad for her first event.

Speed dating was the hot and new alternative to the dating scene. Most of all, it wasn't just for young people. It had a huge age range, from young to old.

Tonight, though, she had arranged a special age grouping, per Mr. Horton's suggestion. Apparently, he had no clue that the age group of twenty-four to thirty-four were the ones too busy to go about dating the conventional way. He had indicated it would be a good way to get her feet wet.

Yeah right. What planet was he from?

Her commission of $1,050 would be a lifesaver in her bank account. She'd had to take a part-time job to make ends meet, and when she'd seen an ad for a speed-dating consultant, after talking to Mr. Horton, they had reached an agreement for her to earn seventy-five percent commission from the profits from each event she held. She had victoriously accepted.

The One Book Store, which she had inherited from her mother, was failing because of a lackluster business. Not many people had been buying paperback books or visiting bookstores over the last couple of years. With e-books and the accessibility to most everything online, bookstores were hard-pressed to make ends meet. Not to mention the big publishers' troubles of not taking returns and not paying the authors their commissions.

Her mother, Nevaeh, had opened the store the year she had given birth to her. Through the years, the three-story brick building had been their workplace and home. The corner lot didn't allow much parking, but the street did.

Smiling, she remembered how her mother had made the place home over the years. It took months, but her mother had built a play area in the small backyard. It had become a project to add on to it from year to year. The area had stayed the same for a couple of years with simply a swing set. Then a picnic table was added with a small garden. Together, they would plant seeds in the spring and harvest vegetables when it was time. The final phase had been the placement of a small bench and a walkway leading up to it from the rear entrance to the building.

A burst of melancholy took over. She checked her phone as a diversion from her emotions. Her grief knotted inside her.

Opaline frowned.

The walkway and bench had been the last change to the backyard. She had done it to honor her mother after she had passed away a month before Opaline's twenty-first birthday.

The building and business, which held all the memories of the two of them, were all she had left of her mother. Now, four years later, she was on the verge of losing it all.

The business.

Her home.

And everything that meant anything to her.

Damn it.

She was going to fight tooth and nail to keep the business afloat. This part-time job would help her financially, but she had to admit that the real reason for taking on the job was to fill her lonely nights. She needed friends. The ones she did have were few and far between and were mostly customers of the bookstore. Plus, she had an alternative motive, which was to hopefully find a man.

The men who visited her store simply weren't her type. Unfortunately, when she thought about what her type of man was, she couldn't pinpoint any specifics.

Tall or short. Easygoing or talkative. Intellectual or funny. Handsome or plain.

There were so many possibilities that she couldn't decide. That could be part of her problem. She didn't know what she wanted in a man. The man she would marry wasn't going to simply be a husband. Her husband would be her life mate or soulmate.

He was out there. She just had to find him and needed some magic to bring him to her.

Opaline snickered. *Magic? Where had that come from? There was no magic in the world, only a person's reality.*

"Bless it be."

She clasped her hand over her mouth, realizing she'd said the words aloud. Anxiously, she looked around to see if anyone had heard. She was alone.

Why had she said those words? Her mother had said them whenever something good had happened but had scolded her when she had used them.

A buzzing sound emitted from her phone, and she tapped off the alarm. She straightened her papers and shoved them into her book bag. Before standing to leave the check-in table, Opaline scanned the area for the last two participants. Not seeing them, she made her way to the bathroom to freshen up before her own speed dates.

It was empty when she entered. She sighed. Her nerves were on edge. As she looked at her reflection, the first thing she saw was her mother's favorite necklace. It was an odd-shaped moonstone with silver accents locking it in place. Her mom had worn it every day after she had gotten sick, saying it gave her strength. Since her mother had passed away, she had begun to wear the moonstone, hoping it would give her strength too.

She thought about touching up the light purple eye shadow but saw it still looked great, and so did her lipstick. Her short white-blonde hair had, for once, stayed curled and framed her face. Turning a little to the right, she wondered if any of the men attending tonight would notice her teal-green-colored blouse, or how the soft yellow tank underneath accented it. Taking a step back, she liked how her low-rider jeans showed off her assets too.

Pleased with how she looked, Opaline left the bathroom. It was time to impress Mr. Right, whoever he was.

two

E amon followed Paula away from the check-in table. He glanced back twice at the beautiful Opaline, who had the greenest eyes he'd ever seen, and smiled inwardly. He had noticed her quick sense of humor, and her laughter had a nice twang to it. He wanted to hear it again. Unknowingly, the corners of his mouth went up a bit. First encounters always had a tendency to leave an impression. And in his line of work, that could be key to solving a murder or a mystery.

"What are you smiling at, bro?"

Had he let slip some emotion? Surprisingly, he had to admit the woman had aroused a long-suppressed feeling.

"I didn't smile."

His sister's laugh told him he hadn't fooled her. Six years was a long time to go without being in a relationship. Opaline might just be someone to get to know better. Having learned to hide his emotions from everyone, he forced his eyebrows upward.

When a person had seen what he had over the years,

you had to close off all emotions. He had become immune to things and people, which was the number one reason he was alone at the age of thirty-two.

"Eamon, look at all these women. You're bound to find someone you might have one thing in common with to ask out."

"This is the last time I agree to do anything you suggest."

Again, she laughed and then took his arm. As they walked into the conference room, he scanned every square inch. The men, he noted, were of an average age and dressed in jeans and dress pants. The women's ages were harder to guess, and they were dressed up for a night on the town.

It seemed like a little bit of night and day between the sexes.

Seeing that he couldn't be the oldest single person in attendance, he relaxed a little. Once again, his police training kicked in, and absently, he counted the number of people in the room. Close to fifty.

He then took a closer look at everyone and recognized some faces from around town, but most of the individuals he didn't know. Having recently moved to Onamia, after his parents and sister had, this was his home now. It was a huge difference from the hustle and bustle in the Twin Cities. It was a lot slower in pace, but he was adjusting and getting used to who the townsfolk were and who the part-timers were.

"What would you like to drink?"

Eamon blinked, reeled in his thoughts, and studied the older bartender for a moment. Tall. In his late fifties. Cold eyes. This seemed strange since the room was filled with people anxious to find someone. Shouldn't the bartender be trying to pick up someone too?

"I'd like a strawberry daiquiri," Paula requested.

"Do you have Summit?"

"No, but I have Miller, Miller Lite, Bud, Bud Lite, PBR, and Premium," the bartender replied.

"I'll take a Premium, thanks," Eamon said. Then he turned and whispered to Paula, "Sis, I'm not sure about this."

"You'll be fine. The women here won't bite, but you'll have to talk fast. And no interrogation-style questions." She chuckled and took her pink drink.

He chose to ignore her comments and grabbed his beer.

"I want to find a table so I can get a good look at all the single men," she said.

Letting her do her thing was the best option for him at this point. He had only agreed to this dating craze so he could get a feel for who lived in town. But the woman at the registration, Opaline, had been intriguing.

Taking a sip of the cold beer, he let the bitter taste hit the spot. Once they sat, he scanned the room again. Four exits. Two in the front, and two in the rear. Tables lined in rows with chairs on both sides. Nothing screamed out at him as a potential problem. He wasn't even sure why he had done that, but it had become a part of who he was. A force of habit.

Eamon cradled the bottle of beer, not really wanting it, and noticed Paula was swiveling in her chair from one side to the other in order to look at everyone.

Taking another drink of his beer, he followed his

sister's action by scrutinizing the people in the room. He focused in on the women, but none caught his attention.

He checked his watch. Had it only been half an hour since he had arrived at the Holiday Inn?

Even now, he wished he had just driven away and not waited for Paula. He had been deep in thought when she had knocked on his car window; he had instinctively reached for his gun. She had been standing next to his car, smiling and waving. He had put on a fake smile, forced himself to relax, and opened the door.

Speed dating. How stupid. What had Paula gotten him into?

He had heard of speed dating but never thought he would take part in an event. When Paula had suggested he sign up, he had laughed.

This was a crock of shit. How could anyone in their right mind talk to someone for a couple of minutes and know if they'd be a good match or not?

Paula had told him to think of it as if he was interrogating someone but with a kind heart. Interrogating people he was good at. He had skills. Whether they worked on this futuristic dating scene was yet to be determined.

"Which questions are good ones to ask?"

"Do I have to hold your hand, bro? Relax. Just enjoy meeting and talking to the opposite sex."

"You're no help. I'm going to leave."

"Oh no, you aren't. Sorry. I forget you haven't dated in a long time." She patted his hand. "I like to ask more personal questions on the first go-around. That way, I can have fun on the second date."

Damn Paula. She had always been able to talk him into anything.

She was right. He was uncomfortable because he wouldn't be in charge. Opening his packet, he took out the suggested list of questions and read them while nursing his beer.

"Look at the first so-called suggested question. What do you do for work? You know I don't like to reveal or talk about being a police detective."

"Then skip that one. Hint, these are only suggestions, not a bible."

"This one is stupid: where are you from? Wouldn't everyone here be from Onamia since we are in a hotel in the heart of the town?"

Paula shook her head and laughed. "You're funny. Maybe some people drove from Little Falls or St. Cloud. Or maybe they moved here from another country. Don't take things so literally."

"I guess I could use that one as an opener."

The more he thought about that question, the more he liked it. He put a check mark next to it. It was simple and to the point. He would be able to reply and say that he lived in town.

The next question he read to himself. *What is one thing about yourself that you'd like to share?* That was another safe one, and he marked that one too. He could reply that he liked funny movies.

After reading question four, he stopped. "Paula, this isn't going to work. One of the questions says I should talk about my last relationship. That isn't going to happen. Why did you talk me into this? No one is going to want to go out with me."

She set down her half-empty drink and looked at him. There was a hint of sadness in her eyes before it disappeared, and she laid her hand on his shoulder. "I care about you. It's time you moved on. Six years is a long time. I just want my fun-loving and easygoing brother back. Even if you don't find anyone interesting tonight, I've accomplished one thing: getting you out and talking to women."

He closed his eyes for a moment. His last relationship had been the most fun-filled four weeks of his life. Losing someone you love wasn't something he liked to talk about. When he opened his eyes, he pushed the darkness away. "You're right. It's time for me to move on, but next time, I'm doing it the old-fashioned way, like going to a bar or pulling over a lady for speeding."

"There he is. Skip questions you feel uncomfortable asking or talking about. Find five or six that will work. You can usually ask three in the five minutes. I recommend having a couple of extras ready in case you have more time. Look at numbers ten, eleven, fifteen, and seventeen. Those all could give you something in common with someone."

"Like I said, if I don't find anyone interesting tonight, you'll have to go barhopping with me," Eamon said.

"Only if you're paying. At least I got you out of the gym and the house. I'm going to mingle. That guy over there is one hunk. See ya." She took her drink and left him alone at the table.

Damn sisters.

He loved Paula, but ninety percent of the time, she was a pain in the ass. She was too good-looking for her own good, and he envied her self-confidence.

He continued watching her, like the good brother he was. Paula approached the clean-shaven man she had pointed out a few minutes earlier. With no fanfare or hesitation, she started talking to him.

Eamon smiled. There was no beating around the bush with her. Full speed ahead for her all the time. He pitied the man who fell in love with her.

The man leaned on the bar, raised his eyebrows slightly, and squared his shoulders before saying hello. From the man's body language, it seemed he was more than interested in Paula. It wasn't much longer before more men joined them at the bar. She was holding court and loved it.

Protective mode clicked in instantly, but he pushed it aside. She was safe. He was within a few feet of her if she did get into trouble. If she did find someone, he could run a check on any dude she wanted to date later as a precaution.

He scanned the room for a third time. It had filled while he'd been trying to figure out which questions to ask. Using the index cards from the welcome packet, he wrote down the questions he'd chosen.

"Excuse me. Excuse me. May I have everyone's attention?"

The room quieted, and Paula returned to their table. The woman who had checked him and Paula in stood at a podium, smiling. The lights surrounding her gave her a heightened radiance, and the air seemed electrified, sending an unexpected spark through him.

"Hello, and welcome. I'm Opaline Lunn, your host. Thank you all for making my very first event a huge success. Who could have guessed that hosting an event in the middle of the week would bring you all out?

"We're going to begin the speed dating session in a couple of minutes. I'd like to thank everyone for participating. We have a very large group tonight: twenty-five men and twenty-five women. Remember, as stated in the speed dating rules, you have five minutes with each person, then you move on to the next date. It's important to stick to the allotted time of five minutes per date, which will be a total of two hours, with one fifteen-minute break after the first hour. Then you will have a half-hour break to socialize. The second round of speed dating, for anyone who is interested in getting to know someone a little more, will start at nine thirty."

"I like the second session the most," Paula said in a low tone to him.

"Shh," he hissed.

"—session will be by request only. Simply mark their names on your list and turn it in at the end of the night. I'll call off those names, and if those people are willing, or wanting, to have another session, they will be given another seven minutes with each person."

"We'll be here all night."

"Good thing we're at a hotel."

"This is hump day."

Laughter, catcalls, and howling erupted.

"I guess that is why the event is held at a hotel," Opaline replied, bringing the crowd under control. "We won't be here all night . . . unless you choose to be."

Another round of lighthearted suggestions was shouted out.

Opaline tapped the mic to silence the crowd. "As I was

saying, if more than two people want another go-around with specific people who agree, the speed dating will start again. This time, the participants will have seven minutes with each person. Any questions?"

"Will we have to pay another thirty dollars for the second session?"

"Good question." Opaline took a sip of water before continuing. "No. This is all part of the speed-dating event. It doesn't matter who takes the lead when you meet. Try to limit your replies so both parties get equal time. Does anyone have any other questions or concerns?"

Paula leaned over to him and whispered, "Have fun."

Before he could reply, Opaline spoke again. "Hearing no other questions, go and have remarkable dates tonight."

Eamon laughed along with everyone else, but he kept his eyes focused on Opaline. She was tall for a woman and had a slender physique. Her white-blonde hair was striking. Loose wisps framed her oval face. Even from where he was sitting, he could see her cheeks had a slight blush to them that wasn't from makeup.

For a moment, Eamon studied her with an intense curiosity. She looked at him. Her green eyes gave her a mysterious façade. She smiled and looked away. His hands began to sweat. A clear sign he was nervous.

But why?

Confused at his body's reaction, he filed it away to be looked at later. Confirming his number, he made his way to his assigned seat and put a check mark next to Opaline's name for a second date.

three

"Do you believe a cup is half-empty or half-full?"
"What makes you laugh?"
"Is sexual compatibility important to you?"
The continuous questioning began to wear on her, and she felt overwhelmed. The men were a blur. Opaline reached for her necklace, rubbing the smooth stone, and waited for the next date.

The blueish moonstone did its trick; her nerves disappeared. Gazing around the room, she relaxed at seeing everyone talking and laughing. The excitement was catching. She realized that, for a first-timer, she was beginning to get the hang of how the five-minute rule worked.

A man in a striped button-down shirt with thick glasses sat down in front of her. "What do you do for fun?"

She smiled. That seemed to be a favorite question among the men. Most would grin after asking it, thinking they were being sexy. But she had come to find that question repulsive. Sometimes their facial expressions were creepy. His look was downright leering and made him unattractive, and along with the question, it was a major turn-off for her.

Not wanting to be rude, she gave him a half-smile, hoping it seemed noncommittal, before replying, "I like to roam around a bookstore."

His disturbing expression instantly changed, and he seemed to be at a loss as to what to say next. When he recovered, he asked, "Do you like mornings or evenings?"

This was the first time she'd been asked this intimate line of questioning. "Mornings," she said cautiously as she checked the time.

"Do you like showers or bubble baths?"

Again, she felt his questions were beyond offensive and too personal for a five-minute date. She made a mental note to let Mr. Horton know and to remove them from the list of suggested questions. Taking a breath before answering, she was saved by the buzzer ending their date, which meant she didn't have to respond and didn't have to ask any of her questions.

"Sorry. On to my next date." Opaline put a large *N* by his name, not finding him interesting, as he shifted to the next seat to her right. It was clear he was looking for one thing tonight: sex—and he thought he was God's gift to women.

She checked her list and saw there was only one more date before the fifteen-minute break, and he had a check-mark by his name.

"Hello again, Ms. Lunn."

She looked up and smiled for real for the first time all night. Eamon.

This was the man who had come in with his sister and had been like a fish out of water at the check-in table. His uncertainty had been kind of sexy in a way. She had caught him staring at her while she'd been making the introductions before the session began. For some unknown reason, this guy fascinated her. She decided to ask questions first.

"Hi, Eamon. Do you want to marry, and have you ever been married before?"

"Yes, and no."

Very interesting.

"What is your most treasured possession, and why?" Opaline didn't look up at him as she waited for his reply, ready to make notes.

"A picture of my mother and father. Why? Because they will always be with me," Eamon said flatly.

A man with deep family commitment. That was a plus and something she hadn't heard all night from the other men. "This is my last question. Do you like pets? Cats?"

"Yes, and yes. Okay, what is your favorite book?"

Opaline met his stare. *Why would he ask her about books? She hadn't seen him at her store before. Did he know who she was?*

She swallowed hard and answered. "It is Dr. Seuss's *Green Eggs and Ham*."

"Who was your hero as a child?"

"Captain Kirk, from Star Trek." She grinned when she saw his surprised look.

"I think I have time for one more question if that is okay with you."

"Of course. Ask away," she said.

"Do you believe in love at first sight?"

"Yes, I do."

At that moment, his sky-blue eyes glistened with a sensuous light. She couldn't help but take a good look at him, taking note of his thick, short black hair that was tapered neatly to his collar. It was still long enough that she could run her fingers through it. His high cheekbones and straight nose were sharp features but gave him a confident air that surrounded him.

She saw that his mouth was curved into a smile, and it reached his eyes, making them squint a little.

Who was this man? He was causing her palms to sweat. An unexpected tingle found its way to the pit of her stomach. Her heart jolted with ripples of excitement. Her pulse quickened to a point, causing her breathing to increase. From the looks of it, Eamon wasn't affected by her at all. He simply sat there, calmly staring at her.

Rubbing her necklace gave her the courage to ask him the same question. "Do you believe in love at first sight?"

"I do, Ms. Lunn."

The buzzer sounded, signaling the halfway point of the first session.

"Excuse me. I can't linger. I have to see to the refreshments." Opaline nearly ran from the table. She didn't know what was wrong with her. When he had replied that he did believe in love at first sight, his rich baritone voice had sent wonderful shivers through her body.

She had hoped to find Mr. Right soon, but this was uncanny. Eamon had unlocked her heart with his one question and reply. An urge to pull him into an embrace and kiss him overcame her. It wouldn't be a friendly kiss on the lips but one that would make him want to take her home.

Hesitating in her rush to get away from him, Opaline stopped midstride. She glanced over her shoulder to see if he had followed, but she instead found a woman in tears.

All thoughts vanished as she struggled to remember the woman's name.

"Ms. Lunn. Ms. Lunn, I have to talk to you."

"Jill, right?"

The woman nodded and wiped her nose with a napkin.

"What's wrong?"

"That man."

Jill pointed to a heavyset man dressed in jeans and a T-shirt that said "Only the Best" on the front.

"You mean Pete?"

"Yes. He shouldn't be allowed here. I've dated him, and he is mean," Jill stated in a hushed tone.

"Mean? In what way?"

"He likes to use force." Jill lowered her eyes in embarrassment. "I was curious and agreed to play his sex games. Bu-but everything got out of hand."

Opaline placed a hand on Jill's shoulder. "Did you report him to the police or to the other speed-dating hostess?"

"No. I was afraid. I conveniently left my table when I saw him coming for our date. I don't think he recognized me. He shouldn't be allowed to participate in any more events or dates."

"Thank you for informing me. I'm sorry about your bad experience. I'll ask my boss, Mr. Horton, what I should do. As far as I know, participants in sexual role-playing activities isn't a reason not to be allowed in a session, unless it was forced or a rape occurred," Opaline said.

She gritted her teeth after saying what she did. It had been the right thing to do, but personally, all she wanted to do was walk over to Pete and kick his ass out the door.

"No, I wasn't raped or forced. I just thought it would

have been more fun. At least you're safe. He only likes to date women with red hair."

"Jill, I'm sorry you had a bad experience. If he tries anything or confronts you tonight, let me know immediately. I hope you find someone more compatible in the second half of the session."

"I do too. I don't have anyone marked for the second session, but I'm hopeful. And please don't let him near me if he marks me as a date."

"I understand. I'll check the lists before making announcements. As always, both parties will have to agree to the second session. Please go and enjoy the refreshments."

"I will. And by the way, you have done a great job." Jill walked away, heading toward the food table.

Opaline stared at Pete and took hold of a string she always carried in her pocket. "So, Pete. You like women with red hair. You need to start caring. I think you should give a rose to all those women you have snubbed with your nose," Opaline mumbled under her breath.

By the time she had finished talking, the string in her pocket had three knots in it. She touched each one and smiled.

Her mother had given her the twelve-inch string and had shown her how to tie the knots with one hand. She had told her to tie the knots whenever she became really mad. This was the first time in a long time that she had tied knots, Opaline realized.

"Is everything okay here?"

She spun around and found Eamon standing next to her. He had briefly placed his hand on her shoulder to get her attention. When he had, she had felt an abnormal electric current in the air. It caused the hairs on her arms to stand up straight, and she shivered a little to shake it.

"Oh my. I didn't know you were next to me." Opaline released the string in her pocket and reached up to her necklace. It was strange to have him so close. His presence was a little disturbing. "There was—is—a little misunderstanding. One of the attendees has dated another attendee previously."

"The woman seemed—no, she had acted—upset," Eamon stated.

"I think you nailed it. Acted is the correct word." Opaline grinned at her play on words. *Had he overheard her and Jill's conversation?*

"She seems to be okay now."

They both looked at Jill, who was standing at the bar next to two men, deep in conversation.

"Yeah, she does."

"I don't want you to think I'm a stalker, but I really enjoyed our five-minute date. I wanted to let you know that I marked your name for the second session." Eamon paused and took a deep breath before adding, "However, I would really like to know if you would go out on a real date with me."

She stared at him. *Is this guy for real? This kind of stuff only happens in books. And she isn't living in a fairy-tale world. Could he be her Prince Charming?*

"Really? You want to go out with me? With me . . . on a real date?"

"Yes. That is, if you would like to."

"Wow. This is my first speed dating event too. I never thought any real dates happened after the fact. I would—"

The buzzer sounded again, cutting off her reply. Everyone began to scramble back to the tables.

"We can talk more later," Eamon said as he walked to his next date.

During her next ten dates, her heart wasn't into asking any of the questions. Opaline found herself searching for Eamon as he went from woman to woman. She noticed that all the women were falling for him. This didn't totally surprise her because she had also fallen for him.

When he was paired with his sister, Paula, she watched his reaction. His face had taken on a sort of admiration and protectiveness. She knew he was someone who would go to extreme lengths to protect what was his. That was a rare quality to be found in a man.

"Ms. Lunn, I can ask a different question if you don't want to answer."

Opaline blinked twice. She had to focus on her date, not on Eamon.

She recognized the man in front of her. His name was Leroy, and he liked historical books. He would come into her bookstore once every two to three weeks to purchase one book. Then, once he had read it, he would come in for another book. He was bald but had a full beard. This always made her laugh, as it was kind of comical. Usually, the men who'd lost their hair made up for it on other parts of their bodies.

"Sorry, Leroy. Did you finish that book on France yet?"

"I did. Thanks for recommending it. I'll be coming in Thursday for something new."

"All right. I'll have a couple ready for you to choose from," Opaline said.

"I think I would like to switch to Russia since some of

the French are intertwined with them," Leroy retorted with excitement.

The buzzer sounded, halting their exchange.

"Okay, Leroy. See you then."

"Thanks, Opaline."

He stood and waved, not concerned that she hadn't answered his preselected questions.

Thankfully, she had gotten out of that screwup nicely. Leroy was nice and friendly. However, he didn't give her any sparks. He really wasn't her type, and she had known that from the conversations they'd had at her store.

The last man on her list for the first session was Owin. He took the empty seat.

"Owin, where are you from?"

He was handsome, had a very short haircut, and seemed a little shy, and that was probably why he was here.

"Around here. I recently changed routes, ma'am. I work for UPS."

"What do you like to do on your day off?"

She was punting here, but it didn't matter. Once again, this guy wasn't her type. Her mind was set on Eamon.

"I work in my garden."

So, he was an earthy type. She gave him points for that and put a little question mark next to his name. He might be someone to consider.

"Do you like to read?"

"I do. As a matter of fact, anything on gardening and horticulture. Books or magazines, it's all good, but—"

"I'm sorry, Owin. We have to cut our date short. I have to get ready for the second session," she said.

"Okay, Ms. Lunn."

"Why don't you stop over to my bookstore, The One Book Store? I'll pull some books for you."

"Thank you. I think your store is on my new route. I'll get to see you often, then."

Opaline smiled genuinely for the second time during the event. Owin was really nice, and she hoped he would, or had, found someone special tonight.

four

Brunettes, blondes, and redheads. This was a candy store for men.

Dismissing the people and the excitement in the room, Eamon tapped his phone in boredom. No messages or calls.

It wasn't like he was expecting any. He was off duty for the night.

He realized none of the women he had dates with mattered. Then he corrected himself. One had.

Opaline.

He was surprised someone had caught his attention in the weirdness of speed dating. A gamut of emotions inundated him.

Confusion.

Joy.

Tension.

They were all feelings he hid from everyone. Finding a table to sit at, he played out the date he had with Opaline in his head. Her nearness, even being across the table from him, had made his senses spin. He hadn't been able to concentrate on his questions or what she had asked.

She had literally run away from him when the buzzer signaled the end of their date and the start of the break. He had followed her in an effort to keep talking to her, wanting to ask her out on a real date, but a woman approached Opaline before he had.

He waited off to the side when he saw that the woman appeared to be crying. He tried not to listen, but his investigation skills and police training kicked in when he heard the woman complain to Opaline about a man named Pete. He had only been able to make out some words, like *cruel* and *sexual*.

Stepping closer, wanting to hear the conversation better, he watched the two women. Opaline had been very nice and sympathetic, telling the woman she would talk to someone named Mr. Horton.

Eamon mentally filed the name Peter to check into some of the town's open and closed cases that involved abusers. Being a new detective on the Onamia police force had its advantages and disadvantages. As far as he could tell, everyone on the team respected him even though he was the new guy.

After the woman had left, he heard Opaline mumble something under her breath. Again, he had strained to hear her but had heard the words *rose, caring,* and *nose.*

When he had touched her shoulder, a shock had rippled through his hand.

What the hell had happened? Rug static?

Even now, thinking it over, his brows drew together as he rubbed his hand. She hadn't reacted to the shock he had given her. How could she have not felt it?

When she had turned to face him, he had read her facial expression like a book. Eamon had seen surprise and anger in the lines on her face.

Opaline hadn't revealed much of her conversation with the other woman, only that she might have been acting. Eamon knew she hadn't lied to him. He had been able to tell by the other woman's eyes and mouth that she hadn't been very upset.

As part of his training and his specialty, reading people's facial expressions and body language was what he did. It came in handy whenever he had to interview suspects.

When he had told Opaline he had put a check mark by her name for the second session and then asked her out on a real date, she had seemed surprised. He had also noted a hint of happiness on her face.

Her action of brushing her hand through her hair was a sign of nervousness. Opaline had simply replied that she would get back to him and had left him standing in the middle of the room.

Sitting at a table alone, nursing his warm beer, Eamon continued to wait for the second half of the first session to start. But an image of Julia, his ex-girlfriend, came to mind from out of nowhere.

He closed his eyes for a moment, realizing their love had been spontaneous, and the pain of losing her had made him vow not to get involved with anyone ever again.

Yet here he was at a speed dating event, finding someone he would like to get to know better. He pushed the melancholy thoughts of Julia away. She was the past, and it was time to move forward. Paula had been right. Moving on was the best thing for him.

Allowing that thought to set his mood, Eamon gazed around the room until he found Opaline. The buzzer sounded at that moment, and everyone was off to find their tables.

"Everyone, please take your seats as soon as possible. The second half of session one is about to begin. Remember, if you have found someone you would like to ask out for a second speed date, mark their name and come see me after this session," Opaline said from behind the podium.

The room turned into a chaotic mess with everyone hurrying, but there was structure to the outcome. He found his table and waited for his date to take her seat as he pulled his file cards with his chosen questions on them from his back pocket.

"Do you like sex in the morning or night?"

No beating around the bush for this woman. "When the mood hits me," he replied.

"What about wearing pajamas?"

"No."

The woman's eyes opened wider, and he grinned. She was interested in him and couldn't hide it. At least not from him.

"Goodness. Direct and to the point. I like that in a man. Beer or wine?"

"Beer." He raised his half-empty glass. "I guess it's my turn. Have you ever fired a gun?"

"No. I don't like them. I wouldn't allow one in my house."

"Okay, then. What about—"

The buzzer cut him off, and he sighed.

As he sat through more dates, it was more of the same. Most of the questions he found during this round were more seductive than during the first half. The favorites among the women had some references to sexual liking. He knew that for the ones who did ask, it was an open invitation to have sex. But he wasn't interested and decided, once again, that speed dating wasn't for him. He found his sister sitting across from him.

"Well, Paula, this is a little awkward."

She reached over and patted his hand. "Yeah, but I'm glad we can talk. How's it going?"

"A little insane. It's crazy but fun, in an odd sort of way. Is there any guy I should be worried about who wants to get to know my little sister better?"

Paula laughed. "Actually, I think so. I've marked him down for the second session. How about you?"

"I have one woman I have marked."

"Only one? I've seen the women looking at you. Eamon, come on. There has to be more than one woman who has caught your attention."

"She's the only one I found who has been honest."

"You and your police methods. Just because you can read people's facial expressions, that doesn't mean you're one hundred percent accurate. Maybe you should just mark off more than one for good measure."

The way Paula's eyes crinkled at the creases distinguished she was teasing him. He let her offhanded comment fly and once again was saved by the buzzer. Glancing at his list, he saw there were only two more dates left.

"Hi, I'm Ebba."

"I'm Eamon."

"Time crunch, here. What do you like to eat?"

He tilted his head to the side. He hadn't expected that

question, and the woman's play on words had him smile. Looking closer at the woman who sat across from him, he noted her long, red, curly hair and brown eyes and that she had a very pretty smile. She wasn't like any of the previous dates.

"I like meat and potatoes."

Ebba beamed, and it made her eyes sparkle. "Do you cook?"

"No," he said.

"Do you like dry wine?"

"Not really."

A disappointed look settled on her face. He was about to add to his last reply because she seemed nice but stopped. He didn't feel the special connection he had with Opaline. Not wanting to string her along, even though she seemed to be an honest person, he proceeded to ask the same questions he had been asking all night long. Just as he was about to ask his final question, the buzzer sounded.

"Thank you, Eamon. I had a nice date."

"Me too."

She stood and walked toward the refreshment table. The room began to get loud with enthusiasm. He noted that couples were starting to form at the bar and tables.

"Excuse me, can I have your attention?" Opaline asked into the microphone. The room quieted, and she continued. "I hope everyone has had some memorable dates. If you have chosen anyone to meet for the second session, please turn in your sheets with your choices. After a fifteen-minute break, I'll call off the names, and if you're interested, please move to the back of the room. I'll have a set of tables and chairs ready for everyone interested in the second round. For those of you who are not wishing to participate or are not chosen, all is not lost. You're invited to stay here and enjoy the bar area or the hotel sports bar restaurant that is also open. Any questions?"

Eamon stayed seated and observed everyone while Opaline talked. He folded his piece of paper, with only her name marked by his, and stood.

"Okay, how many names did you add?"

Paula's question didn't deserve a reply, but he did answer as he laid his paper down. "None."

"You're hopeless, big bro. I have five. I think a couple of the guys marked my name too. I might get a couple of good dinners out of this."

"Sis, that's not right."

Her laughter caught him off guard for a moment, and he realized she was kidding. How he had misread her, he didn't know.

"Get me another beer before the second session."

"Sure, no problem," Paula replied.

He scanned the room for Opaline but couldn't find her. In his search, he spotted the man named Pete talking to Ebba. That was not good, if the man was trouble. His instinct to protect took hold, and he walked over to them.

"Hi, Ebba. We were cut short by the buzzer, and I wanted to ask you a question."

Pete looked at him and immediately excused himself. That was the action of a guilty man. He was definitely going to have to investigate Pete later.

Ebba's eyebrows rose, forming a couple of lines on her forehead as she spoke. "Sure. What would you like to know?"

"You had asked me about cooking, and it got me thinking. Do you own a restaurant?"

"Yes, I do. It's called Mignon's Place, right on Main Street. Have you been a customer of mine?"

"No, but after we talked, I thought I recognized you. I saw your picture in the paper," Eamon said.

"Oh, that." She laughed and looked downward. "When you do decide to come to try out my restaurant, let me know. It will be on me."

"That's really nice of you. I wasn't looking for a free meal, but since you offered and I don't cook, it would be a nice treat."

They both laughed.

"I will do that. I hope you have a good evening."

"I just did. It was nice meeting you, Eamon."

He walked to the table where Paula was sitting, with his beer waiting for him, and joined her to wait for the second session. His gaze combed the room for Pete, but he was nowhere to be found.

"What was that all about?"

"Nothing," Eamon mumbled as he took a sip of his beer. "Did you know she is the owner of that restaurant on Main Street?"

"Oh, I thought I recognized her. I've eaten there. The food is awesome."

He let his sister talk, but he didn't pay attention as he saw Opaline working on getting the next session ready. As he watched her, all he could concentrate on was getting her to go out on a real date with him.

five

Opaline took out her phone during the break and posted a picture on Facebook with a status: *We had dates! Did you?*

She smiled. It had a clever hook for her next event in two weeks. Mr. Horton, who had the entire Northern-Midwest territory of Minnesota, had said the previous coordinator held an event every two months, sometimes every three. One of his requirements for the position was that he wanted someone to really push the speed dating. She had assured him that she was the right person to host several events. He had seemed pleased with her enthusiasm and was always pleasant in his emails when they corresponded.

Her eyebrows drew together. *Why hadn't we met each other in person yet?* Her interview and conversation had all been via email.

Pushing those thoughts away, she checked the list of people wanting a second session. Opaline cut and pasted the Excel worksheet to form a new list with everyone's names and assigned them new numbers.

A weird sense of excitement set in as she saw four men were wanting another date with her, and one of them was Eamon. He, on the other hand, had three women wanting dates with him besides herself, but he had only marked one name. Hers.

Then she remembered she hadn't given him her answer about going out on a real date. Should she go out with him?

Her mind screamed yes.

Any man who believed in love at first sight was definitely worth the time for a real date. She didn't have to convince herself to go out with him. It was plain and simple logic. She liked him, so her answer would be yes.

Looking up from her computer, she searched for Eamon and found him sitting with his sister. Their eyes met for a moment. She shifted her glance back to her keyboard after seeing the heat in his gaze and fought the urge to look over at him again.

Opaline forced herself to concentrate on the spreadsheet and managed to complete it, clicking Save as she shut the laptop. Slipping her phone into her wristlet purse, she headed to the restroom to pull together her wild emotions. She went into an empty stall and heard a couple of women talking as they came in after her.

"Did you see that guy with the huge biceps?"

"I did."

There was some laughter and then the sound of water running. Not wanting them to know she was in one of the bathroom stalls, Opaline stayed quiet.

"That T-shirt he was wearing left nothing to the imagination."

"I know. I wanted to run my hands all over that firm chest of his. I marked his name for the next session."

"I did too. I hope he accepts. I think he would be wonderful in..."

The women's voices faded, and Opaline put her hand on the latch, but a new set of voices took over. Continuing to be quiet, she waited for the new group of women to leave.

"This is fab. I'm glad I came."

"Me too. I wonder when the next event will be."

"Next one? Didn't you say you found someone tonight?"

"Yeah, but it can't hurt to keep looking."

The women's laughter echoed in the bathroom and then came the sound of the door shutting. Opaline couldn't help but smile.

She was a success. *Goodness alive.*

Mr. Horton should be pleased with her performance. And if her figures were correct, this would be the easiest cash she had ever made. If she did do one a month, the extra income would be a real blessing and help with all the bookstore's expenses and the mortgage. She could be debt-free with some additional cash in the bank.

She sighed. She knew better than to count on things before they happened.

One day at a time. That had become her motto since her mother had become sick and died.

Her phone buzzed from inside her wristlet, signaling she had five minutes before the next session began.

Opaline exited the stall, freshened up her lipstick, and fluffed her hair.

Her pending dates had her wondering what kind of questions they would ask. Would Eamon stick to things they might have in common?

Then she recalled one of Mr. Horton's emails, warning her that during the second session, things could get more personal. Did that mean Eamon would ask her more intimate questions? Or should she take the lead and ask them?

No. She wanted their date to be spontaneous, not a planned-out, question-and-answer session. She touched her necklace. Her Mr. Right was out there, and if it turned out to be Eamon, he still had to prove that it was him.

Opaline refused to dwell on reasons why he couldn't be the one for her or if the universe was trying to tell her something. She reentered the ballroom and smiled. The room was still filled with many of the attendees, all of them mingling and talking. The snack table she saw had been hit hard. She made a mental note to get more food for the next event.

Her phone buzzed. It was time to start the next session.

Opaline grabbed the microphone. "Excuse me. May I have your attention?"

As she waited for the room to quiet down, she saw Eamon toward the back of the crowd. He grinned when their eyes met. She returned his smile, feeling an attraction to him, even from a distance.

The noise level lowered, and she lifted the mic. "I wanted to thank everyone for making my first speed-dating event a huge success." Opaline paused due to the applause and the whistling. "If anyone is interested, I'll be hosting another speed dating night in two weeks. Please sign up if you'd like to attend or visit my Facebook page, *OM-SPEEDDATING*, and ask to be my friend to ensure you receive an invite."

The noise level upped again so she tapped the microphone.

"Thank you. Now I'm going to read the names for the second session. If your name is called and you would like to participate, please move to the back of the room. Remember, in this session, you are allowed seven minutes per date. Here we go."

Opening her laptop, she began to read the twenty-seven names, including her own. When she finished, she saw that most of the attendees had accepted and were waiting in the back of the room.

"For those of you not having a second date, your night is over. Have a nice night and thank you again. I hope to see you at the next event."

Setting the mic down, she took her bottled water and laptop and joined the others at the back of the room.

"Okay, so this part gets tricky. I'll call the woman's name and then her dates. If your name is called more than once, please finish your first date before going on to the next one. Remember, seven minutes. We'll start in five, so please take your seats."

She took her assigned seat number and waited. Seeing that everyone was ready before the five minutes were up, she pushed the buzzer, signaling the start of the second session.

Her three dates came and went. None of them held a candle to her upcoming date. She shook her head at some of the questions she'd been asked.

"Do you like to shower together?"

"Do you cook in the nude?"

"Do you pick your toenails?"

"Do you like green M&M's?"

Personal wasn't the right word for those questions. They had a sexual undertone to them but not enough to be lewd. The toenail question had been the weirdest, and she had laughed aloud. However, she regretted doing that when she saw the man's face. He had been dead serious. She had quickly replied no and excused herself from the table, faking that she had received a phone call.

Now she was waiting for her fourth and final date, Eamon.

Goodness, anticipation is everything.

She couldn't believe he wanted to go out with her on a real date. Most guys found her too intellectual. It wasn't her fault she owned a bookstore and loved to read. History, fiction, romance, fantasy, sci-fi—it didn't matter. Everything was interesting to her. No genre was off-limits.

The buzzer sounded, and she waited for Eamon. He arrived and took his seat. He didn't say anything. She didn't either. They sat for a moment, looking at each other, his blue eyes to her green eyes.

Abruptly, the air surrounding her turned hot, but it wasn't the kind of hot that made you sweat. It was the kind of sexual intensity that could consume a person, only to let go once it had been satisfied. Opaline fought the urge to fan herself.

Like a foggy night, the room around the two of them became hazy. Eamon reached across the table and touched her cheek. Her body had a will of its own, and she leaned into his hand, closed her eyes, and waited for him to kiss her.

"Opaline? Opaline, are you all right?"

"Wha-what?"

The room was clear again when she opened her eyes. Eamon hadn't kissed her. She had imagined the kiss. He hadn't reached out to her. But he was now. He didn't touch her cheek. like she had envisioned. Instead, he was touching her hand. Until he wasn't.

Goodness sakes alive.

"Sorry. I guess the excitement of the night has gotten to me," she said, recovering. "Did you ask me something?"

"No problem. I asked what you like to eat. If we're going to go out on a date, I'll have to find a restaurant because I don't cook."

"I haven't technically agreed to go out with you." She laughed nervously.

"I'm not going to let you say no."

"Oh, is that how it's going to be?" Opaline reached across the table and took his hand. "I guess I don't have a choice, then. Yes, I would like to go out with you."

"Great. Does tomorrow night work for you?"

"You do work fast," she said, lowering her voice, which came out in a low silvery tone.

"Only when I need to."

She knew he was implying other things, and she smiled again, wishing he had kissed her.

The buzzer ended their date, and Opaline stood. Most of the other attendees had finished their dates too. "I hate to rush things, but I need to wrap things up for the event."

"If you would like, I can help you with the cleanup," Eamon said.

"That's so thoughtful, and here I was thinking you only liked to give the orders."

She saw by the way his head tilted to the side that her reply had caught him off guard. He looked like a kid caught with his hand in the cookie jar, and he was having a hard time coming up with a comeback. He mustn't be used to word games like her customers at the bookstore were. They usually gave it right back to her. Eamon, on the other hand, was still at a loss for words.

"Yes, I'd love your help. I have to stick around until everyone leaves. I'll make an announcement to let them know what time we have to be out of here. Then I can—no, we—can start."

"Sounds good. I'll round up my sister to pitch in too," he said.

Opaline heard him chuckle and wondered if he had offered his sister's help without her knowledge. She walked over to the microphone and tapped it to get everyone's attention. "Hello again. Or should I say good night? I'm sorry to be the bearer of bad news, but we only have the room until eleven o'clock. So if I can have everyone start to move out, that would be great. The hotel has a bar and grill that is open until one o'clock if you want to continue your date in there."

The crowd moaned, but everyone started to exit. Overall, they looked happy as they did.

About twenty minutes later, Paula, Eamon, and herself were left, plus a few of the hotel staff.

"That went smoothly," Paula said.

"It sure did. Thanks for the help. All that is left to do is pack up my stuff and pay the hotel," Opaline stated.

"Great. Sounds like I'm free to go, then." Paula looked

at Eamon, who nodded. "I'm going to the bar and grill. Scott, one of my dates, is waiting for me."

"Text me when you leave and when you get home. And I don't want you going home with anyone," Eamon said.

"Come on. You know I won't." Paula smiled sweetly.

Opaline laughed at seeing Paula's fingers crossed behind her back.

"Show me your hands, sis," Eamon demanded.

Paula turned to reveal her hands, which still had her fingers crossed.

"I'm serious. No overnights 'til I can check the guy out."

Paula's smile disappeared. "Okay, bro, but that goes for you too." She waved at them as she strutted out of the ballroom.

"I'm sorry, Opaline. I'm just very protective."

"I don't have a problem with that. And was that an invite for me to spend the night at your house?"

Her teasing reply provoked a shocked look from Eamon, but only for an instant before a sparkle lit up his blue eyes.

"You're as bad as my sister, Ms. Lunn."

"Should I take that as a compliment?" His use of her full name had her wondering if she had overstepped, and she berated herself for doing so.

"You'll have to ask her."

Opaline laughed, thankful it appeared she hadn't been too presumptuous. Their conversation took on a new direction to how the event had turned out. Side by side, they walked to the hotel's registration desk.

Once she paid the bill, she turned to Eamon. "Thank

you for helping with cleaning up the room and for the two great dates."

"You're welcome. And it's me who should thank you. Can I walk you to your car?"

His earlier comment about being protective came back to her. She found his offer gracious and wondered if he was this way with all the women he dated.

"That would be great. But I don't have a car. I drive an SUV."

"Interesting. I took you for a sports car type of woman."

He retrieved a couple of her bags from the floor. She shook her head as they walked to her blue Chevy Tahoe, feeling as if they had done this a hundred times. "Well, this is my baby."

Pressing her key fob, the doors unlocked. Eamon put her bags into the back seat. She closed the door and turned. Eamon was right next to her.

"Opaline, I've wanted to kiss you all night. May I?"

What a gentleman.

His presence was soothing and sensual at the same time. She nodded and emptied the space between them. He placed his hands on her arms, drawing her closer, and lowered his head. Her senses were out of control. She closed her eyes, waiting for his lips to cover hers.

She felt his breath on her lips first, then his mouth. Firm but soft. His lips brushed against hers lightly. Then they were gone. Opening her eyes, she found him staring at her. A desire so drugging filled her with a craving.

She wanted more.

As she slid her arms over his chest, she initiated the second kiss. Their mouths hungrily searched each other's.

This was a kiss like no other. Her body pressed against his. She wanted something more.

Then his mouth left hers, and a cool breeze brushed her now-swollen lips. "Oh, my goodness."

"Opaline, I..."

"Don't," she said, placing a finger on his lips. "I wanted this too."

"I would never force or press you to do something we both might regret later. The gentleman in me has resurfaced and knows that an invite to my place would be inappropriate at this time."

"I agree." She released her hold on him, and he did the same. Stepping out of his arms, she found the circle of comfort they had provided had vanished. "We never settled on a time for our dinner date tomorrow."

Eamon took her hand into his, and she felt her pulse begin to quicken. Was he going to kiss her again? She wanted him too.

"Should we say six thirty? I'll pick you up."

"That's a little old-fashioned. I can meet you."

"Then it wouldn't be a true date," he said.

"Fine. Pick me up at six thirty. My address is 104 Main Street."

"Got it," Eamon stated. He leaned in and kissed her.

This time, she was breathing heavily when they finished. He released her hand and opened the truck door for her. She climbed in and waved goodbye.

As Opaline pulled away, she couldn't help but glance in the rearview mirror for one last look at the most amazing thing that had come her way in a very long time.

A man named Eamon.

six

Opaline's blue Tahoe disappeared down the street and turned onto Main Street. Eamon smiled with self-assurance and walked over to his car.

Sweet. She had kissed him. He hadn't lost his touch with women after all.

"Well, well, big bro. I see you scored tonight."

Stopping midstride, he looked over his shoulder to find Paula heading toward him. How had he missed seeing her in the parking lot?

She came up to him and gave him a hug.

"Why did you hug me? I didn't score. I merely kissed a woman. So what?"

"That *is* considered scoring," Paula said.

"If kissing a woman is scoring, I guess I have done it a lot. The new slang, however, is lost on me. I'm old school. In my day, scoring was going all the way with a girl. And if you're wondering, Opaline and I are going to have a real date tomorrow."

"What? Opaline and Eamon, sitting in a tree, k-i-s-s-i-n-g—"

"Paula, stop. You are acting childishly."

"I'm going to have to start calling you a player soon." She laughed.

Eamon pressed his lips together, forming them into a thin line. He knew what the term *player* meant. He definitely didn't fit into that category where women were concerned. Nor would he ever. Why would she have said that?

"I am not a player." He emphasized each word. If she had been one of his fellow officers, she would know not to press him any further.

"Calm down, Eamon. I'm kidding. Walk me to my car. That guy, Scott, who I thought was worth my time, wasn't."

"Did he do something to you?" Gone was his anger at Paula. It was now centered on the man named Scott. He looked around to see if he could find the man. "Where is he?"

"No, no, he didn't do anything. I checked his Facebook page during break and found out he is a player. But don't worry. I'm going to ask Opaline to poke someone else for me."

"Poke? As in Pokey and Gumby?"

"You're weird, bro. That's so old school. No one knows who that is anymore. A poke is when you send a message to someone you are interested in. That person can send you a poke back, and you're the only two people who can see what you are saying."

"Technology is changing so fast that I can't keep up. And what's up with all the dating apps? Can't a guy simply meet a woman at a bar, or on the street, and ask her out?"

Paula giggled and patted him on his shoulder. "It's okay. I'll have you up to par in no time."

"Sure. Whatever."

She slid her arm into his as they walked to her car. Who did she think she was? He didn't need any coaching. He had done pretty well on his own with getting Opaline to go out with him.

Old school, my ass.

When they reached Paula's car, she hugged him again and kissed his cheek before getting into her car. "I'm glad you moved here. It's nice having you around. Love ya, bro."

"Those are some smooth words, but you still have to text me when you get home."

"Right. Text when I arrive home."

Like before, he watched a car leave the parking lot. Then he was alone for the second time that night. His thoughts turned to Opaline as he realized he hadn't gotten her phone number. She had given him her address; that was good. But what if something came up and he had to cancel? He wouldn't be able to get a hold of her.

He had two options: One, use the police computers to get her phone number. Or second, look up The Book Store and call her at work.

Pushing the unlock button on his keys, the car's lights flashed, and a beep sounded. With his hand on the door handle, a burst of cold wind swirled around him. Dirt and leaves flew into the air. He squeezed his eyes shut and shivered.

Damn late-spring winds, he thought.

He wiped his eyes before opening them. When he did,

he looked upward. The clear night sky from moments ago was gone. Ominous dark clouds now filled the sky. Being so close to Mille Lacs Lake gave Onamia a lot of unpredictable weather problems.

He was about to open his car door when his phone rang, the ringtone playing *"Bad Boys. Bad Boys. Whatcha gonna do?"*

Shit.

He tapped the Accept button. "Detective Dayan."

"Sir, we have a break-in at 104 Main Street. The closest officer on duty is about a half an hour away. I know you're off duty, but are you able to take this call?"

One zero four. That was the address Opaline had just given to him.

"Yes, I'm on my way. Get dispatch to confirm the address."

Inside his car, he saw the police dispatcher had already sent over the address to his computer. Without hesitation, Eamon flicked on the police lights and pushed the gas pedal to the floor.

All he could think about was Opaline. *Is she all right? Is she scared? Does she have any family he can call?*

Then his thoughts took a new course. It had to have been an inside job.

Fuck.

Could one of her employees be unhappy? Or could one of her customers who knew she would be at the speed-dating event have taken advantage of her store being empty?

No, not just her customers but everyone on Facebook was now a suspect. Then he remembered the man named Pete from the speed dating event had gone missing.

A rush of anger overtook him. If that man, Pete, was involved or if he had hurt Opaline, he was never going to see daylight again.

Eamon took the turn onto Main Street too fast, and the car's tires squealed. He floored it again and then slammed on the brakes when he approached The One Book Store. He put the car into park. In a fluid motion, he opened his door and reached down for his 9 mm Glock. Using the car door as protection and his gun drawn, he surveyed the area.

The building had its front window broken, and the front door stood wide open.

"Opaline! Where are you?" he shouted.

No sound. No reply.

"Damn it, Opaline, answer me!"

Still nothing.

It was time to move, and he did so slowly. Looking to the left and right with his gun pointed, he proceeded inside through the open door.

Bookshelves were overturned and the books were thrown carelessly around. He stepped over them and made his way to the counter. Going low, he searched behind the counter and found the cash register untouched.

With his back to the wall, he assessed the damage. Broken glass and books were all over the place and looked to be the extent of the destruction the perpetrator had done.

He was about to call out to Opaline again when he heard odd sounds coming from the rear of the store. Moving cautiously around the downed shelves, he paused to hear the sounds.

He flicked his head to the right when a new round of noise erupted in the silence. It was coming from behind a curtain. Cautiously, he approached the thick fabric and flung it aside. Instead of a person, it revealed a doorway with another curtain.

Where was Opaline? Was she making the sounds, or was it the intruder?

He took a deep breath when he realized his emotions were getting the better of him. That never happened. He knew better.

A scratching sound vibrated from behind the second curtain. Time wasn't his friend here if the goal was to find Opaline. He debated his next course of action in his head.

Should he call out to Opaline for a third time? Or do this by the book and call out that he was the police?

His emotions won. He was on a mission to find Opaline. Taking hold of the curtain, he led with his gun and stepped around the fabric.

A dim light revealed a staircase leading up to a second level. Moving up the stairs one at a time, he reached the closed door. He could still hear the sounds.

"Police!" Eamon yelled and pounded on the door.

The sounds ceased, and he heard footsteps. Repositioning his gun, he readied himself for the unexpected and waited for the door to open. His adrenaline was off the charts when the darkened staircase was flooded with light.

"Police!" he yelled again as a white fur ball ran by his legs and down the stairs.

"Athena, come back here. I'm sorry. Did she scare you, Officer?"

"Opaline?

"Yes, can I help you, Officer?"

"Didn't you hear me yell your name?"

"Eamon?"

He could see she was confused. He lowered his gun and stepped through the doorway, very relieved to see she was unharmed. "Yes."

"What are you doing here? Why were you pointing a gun at me?"

"Sorry about that. Are you okay? Did you find a perpetrator in here when you got home?"

"No. The front window was broken, and the door had been kicked in. I came upstairs and found my home trashed too and called the police. I'm confused. Why are you here?"

"I'm the police. Actually, I'm Detective Dayan. I'm on the Onamia police force."

"What?"

He holstered his gun. The white fur ball from earlier rushed past him again, back into the apartment. "I guess this is my fault. I usually don't tell people right off the bat that I'm a detective. It tends to scare them away. After you left, I got the police call that there'd been a break-in. I recognized the address as the one you had just given me. I was the closest so I came here."

"My goodness, this is interesting."

"Are you sure you're alright?" He took her hand into his, and everything became brighter, more vibrant.

"Yeah. I'm just pissed off. This is going to cost me a lot of money, which I don't have, and time to put my store back together." She withdrew her hand to tuck a strand of hair behind her ear. Instantly, the colors inside the room darkened as if someone had turned off the light.

"I'm pretty good with a hammer and nails. That is, if you need someone to help."

Opaline smiled, but it didn't reach her eyes. He could

see the stress was getting to her. From his experience, Eamon knew that trauma hit a person at this point, and they broke down. He didn't wait for it to hit her full force and pulled her into his arms close and kissed her forehead. She wrapped her arms around him and laid her head on his chest.

"Eamon, why would somebody do this? I've seen some of the work when kids vandalize places here in town, but this doesn't seem they had done it. I have plenty of valuables sitting around in my apartment, and none of them were taken. Even the cash register wasn't broken into, and I keep fifty dollars in it."

"Everything will be okay."

"I don't understand why this happened."

Over the top of her head, he surveyed the room. Seeing a couch, he led her over to it, sensing Opaline's emotional stress was about to break. They sat, and he continued to keep his arm around, trying to calm her. The white cat followed them and jumped into her lap, purring.

"I'm saddened by all this. It's my home. I'm so pissed. Whoever did this has to be twisted. I hope he, or they, broke a bone, or bones, as karma for their evilness."

A sudden swish of heat engulfed him. The lights flickered, and the colors of everything once again brightened for a millisecond.

What was going on?

He blinked several times. Opaline stared at him with a surprised look. Had she felt the heat too? Had she seen the bright colors?

Meow. Meow. Meow.

The cat's very vocal, drawn-out cry at not getting the

attention she required broke their connection, and he looked away.

"Athena, what's wrong, girl?" Opaline lifted the cat onto her shoulder and spoke to it like a child. The soothing words worked. The cat quieted and leaped down to lay on the floor and stare at them.

"Oh my. The furnace must've kicked on. It is getting warm in here," she said as she fanned herself with her hand.

That must be why he was perspiring. He wiped some off his forehead. "It did get warm." As he turned to look at her, he knew the furnace wasn't the cause of his discomfort. It was her. She was so beautiful, even with her eyes glistening with unshed tears. Her lips trembled slightly in an erotic way. They were teasing him. All he could think about was kissing her.

"Excuse me, Detective Dayan. What do you want us to do?"

The male voice put the brakes on his unprofessional thoughts, and he stood, moving away from the couch and Opaline. In the doorway were two plain-clothed officers. "You guys made good time."

"We did, sir. Should we put out an APB on a suspect?"

"No. Warren, see if you can find a weapon and get any fingerprints you can. Thomas, get someone over here to board up the windows and get the lights on. I'll be down in a minute."

They acknowledged his orders and left. Eamon turned back toward Opaline and saw her cat had taken his spot on the couch. She sat with one hand petting the cat and the other wiped at tears that had begun to fall.

"Opaline, is there someone I can call?"

"No, I don't have any family."

"I'm calling my sister, Paula. You stay up here."

Taking out his phone, he texted Paula, asking her to come over to Opaline's bookstore immediately. Not waiting for a reply, Eamon shoved the phone into his pocket, and without taking a look at Opaline, he headed downstairs.

His protectiveness slithered forward for the second time in less than twelve hours. Determination set in. *Whoever did this to Opaline is going to pay dearly,* he vowed.

seven

Using the shadows as a cover in the backyard of The One Book Store, Alyaaluladonati stood frozen for a moment. An eerie quiet surrounded him, and his senses heightened as he narrowed in on the energy.

Trouble.

Unable to shake the feeling, he ran toward the fence as police cars arrived. With one hand on the top rung, ready to climb over it, his body jerked, and he fell to the ground.

Incapable of moving, he moaned. Intense pain surged through his arms and hands. He clamped his lips together, shutting out his screams.

He maneuvered his body the best he could without the use of his arms to lean against the fence, immobilized. Waves of pain consumed him. Slowing his breathing to quiet his mind, he concentrated on what had just happened.

Someone had put a spell on him. The question was who.

His arms hung limp by his side, and his fingers were protruding at odd angles. Another wave of agony cascaded within him. Alyaaluladonati turned his head to the side and threw up.

He centered in on the searing pain as he propped himself against the fence and realized that every bone in his hands and arms was broken. Directing his gaze the best he could to the building he had just ransacked, he saw a lone figure standing in front of a large window.

Opaline.

He knew it was her by the blue-and-silver aura that surrounded her, even if he couldn't see her face. That aura was how he had located her. It had taken years, but he had done it. Her energy rays were strong tonight. She was so much more powerful than her mother had been at this age. Unknowingly to Opaline, her powers had evolved.

He wondered how the little bitch had cast a spell when she didn't know she could. All these past years, he had watched Opaline growing up, not knowing she was a witch. What could have triggered her powers?

This was a huge game changer if she was coming into her abilities.

His plans that he had fostered into fruition had taken over 150 years to develop. After being stranded here on this godforsaken parallel plane, he had studied and watched for the right witches to come along.

Twenty-six years ago, he had met three women who had shown such promise: Olex, Neveah, and Eeva. However, they hadn't been as strong as he needed them to be. Taking matters into his own hands, he had impregnated them all at the same time and waited for their daughters to be born. At their births, he briefly experienced the true power of a mother's and daughter's connection. All six of them would have given him enough energy to take himself home.

But the three witches had tricked him. When they found out he had used them only to get the babies and planned to kill them all to transfer their powers to him, they placed binding spells on the girls and themselves to hide.

Alyaaluladonati watched as Opaline reached up to touch something that was hanging from her neck.

There it was. One piece of the three that was required to initiate his own spell to leave this place.

Damn it. No wonder he hadn't found it in her house. He had suspected Olex, Nevaeh, and Eeva had given their daughters the stones they had stolen. He could feel it calling him now.

Confident that he was steps closer to gathering the three stones, he grinned. All he had to do was find his other two daughters and their stones. Once in his possession, he could complete the spell, which would drain them of their powers and send him to his true place in time.

A figure joined Opaline at the window, and things began to make sense. The male next to her had to be her source of conjuring that had triggered her powers and had broken the binding spell. If her powers were unrestricted, it was just a matter of time for the other two to find their way here. The three had always found their way to each other, no matter how far apart they were. He had found over the years that it was the same at each juncture of the witches. One became two. Two became three. Then the three were depleted.

Clearing his mind, he whispered, "Beware, little one. I

have begun the hunt. I will beat you to the punch. No one gets the best of me, Alyaaluladonati. Now, undo the bump. Because I have won."

It was a simple slew of words, but it was all he needed. The bones in his hands began to heal, reshaping themselves to their correct positions. The new pain they were creating was worse than when the original spell had done its damage.

He groaned and held his breath.

When his counter spell had done what it was supposed to do, he rose to his feet. He took one last look at Opaline, who still stood by the window overlooking the backyard, and then he walked into the darkness, leaving a trail of mist behind him.

eight

Opaline chose to not listen to Eamon's instructions for her to stay upstairs and went to see what everyone was doing. She was met with swirling red, white, and blue lights, which added more drama to her trashed store.

There were police officers inside and outside. She didn't know Onamia had so many. From the bottom of the stairs, she searched for Eamon.

She found him talking to other officers by the front entrance. How had she missed the fact that Eamon was a police detective? What were the odds that a man she had just met, and sort of liked, would show up at her door, pointing a gun at her?

It had been nonsensical at the time, but now, as she recalled the scene in her mind, it had been scarier than Fright Fight on the Syfy channel.

Meow. Meow.

"Hello, Athena. What's going on? Do you want some love?"

Meow. Meow.

Opaline cuddled Athena, her long-haired ragdoll cat, to her body, thinking of the moment when Eamon had held her a few minutes ago. All her fears and anger about the break-in had faded away. His arms had been so strong, and his chest had been firm, just like in the parking lot when they had kissed.

But something quirky had happened when they had stood in each other's arms. The air around them had become crushingly sweltering. It had caused her to perspire, which never happened. It had only lasted a second or two, and when they released each other, her body temperature had returned to normal.

She grinned at how absurdly her night had played out. She had arrived home to find The Book Store's front door open, and the large front window broken. Then she had waited for the police, only to have Eamon arrive and point a gun at her.

Even her horoscope—which she read every day—had said that love, power, and friendship will become one today. It had sounded generic, like they did most days, but it now took on a new meaning as she reflected on all the events that had played out today.

"Oh, Miss Athena, when I find love, which might be right in front of us, I'll make sure I find you a mate too," she said as she continued to pet her.

She couldn't take her eyes off Eamon, who was still talking to some officers. He stood with his hands on his hips and occasionally moved one hand to the back of his neck. He would rub it for a moment and then return it to his hip. The officers, she noticed, gave him the kind of respect that was earned and not just given.

Shifting her gaze from Eamon, she saw some of her customers standing on the street. As she was about to go back upstairs, she noticed Paula and Ebba, the woman who owned the restaurant at the other end of the street, come to the store's front door, which now had yellow caution tape on it.

Her eyebrows drew together in confusion. She had known Paula would be coming, but why would Ebba be here? She had only met her twice, once before at a town meeting and then during the speed dating event.

Eamon lifted the yellow tape and motioned for them to come in. The two women ran through the store, sidestepping the fallen bookshelves and books to reach her, causing Athena to jump out of her arms.

Paula reached her first and was out of breath as she took her hands into hers. "Opaline, are you okay?"

"Yeah. I found my store like this." She waved her arms at the mess, and then the tears began to fall. Her beautiful store was trashed. The sitting area her mother had loved to use was the worst. The deep red, plush couch had been slashed. All the brightly colored pillows had been ripped open and unstuffed. The white fluff lay all over the room, giving it a weird look as if it had snowed. The quartz crystal lamp that had stood in the corner was broken, and the pieces glittered like tears on the floor. The magnificent lavender curtains that had hung on each side of the entryway had been pulled down and slit too.

"Hi. We met tonight. I'm Ebba. I own the restaurant down the street on the corner. I saw all the police cars and came right over to see if I could help."

"Thanks for coming. I'm just not sure what to do—or

where to begin. This has never happened before," Opaline said. She couldn't stop the tears that fell down her cheeks.

"Oh, honey, you've been very brave and strong. No one should go through this by themselves. Come over to my restaurant. I'll fix us something to eat. Paula, you can get the coffee started for the officers," Ebba stated.

"I can't—I can't leave Athena."

"Who's Athena?" Both Paula and Ebba asked at the same time.

"My cat."

"Bring her too. Not that I have mice, but she's more than welcome in my place anytime. Just don't tell the health inspector."

Athena appeared at their feet out of nowhere, purring and weaving herself between their legs. Opaline picked her up and allowed Paula and Ebba to lead her away. Outside, she glanced at Eamon. He smiled and nodded at her. That's all it took. Her heart skipped a beat, and she stopped in her tracks.

Goodness, what is wrong with her? Who falls for a guy in one night?

His kiss in the parking lot had been powerful and sexy. She could only think of being close to him. He had made her feel safe. Pivoting her feet in his direction, she was stopped by Paula.

"You have it good, girl. Now is not the time to go to him. By the way, I had a fabulous time tonight at speed dating," Paula said.

Eamon had turned away from them, and the draw to be close to him was lost. Tightening her hold on Athena, she blinked and refocused on walking.

"I'm glad you did. I might have to schedule more of

them now. I'll need the cash to fix my store," Opaline stated.

"Sorry to say I had just an okay time." Ebba sighed. "I didn't find anyone who liked to cook. I will be looking forward to the next one too."

"You mean to tell me, with your good looks and ability to cook, you couldn't find anyone with something in common with you?"

"Nope. Not a single soul."

Opaline exchanged a look with Paula, who shrugged her shoulders.

"I did find someone. I was going to email you, Opaline. I want you to poke him for me," Paula said.

"As administrator, I can do that. Getting people together is part of my job. Send me his name."

They waited for Ebba to open the doors to her restaurant, Mignon's Place, and walked inside.

"The lights are next to the fake fern," Ebba announced.

Having never been inside the restaurant before, Opaline found she liked the interior. The main dining room was painted in hues of blue, just like her store. The tablecloths would have matched her now ruined curtains. And on each table sat a little quartz crystal stone lamp. *It's uncanny that they decorated their businesses with the same taste,* she thought.

"I love the place. Who was your decorator?"

"Thanks. My mother. She was an interior designer before she died."

"Found the switches," Paula said.

The area became encased in light. Athena meowed as if she had just given her approval. She jumped from

Opaline's arms, climbed onto a golden-colored couch in the waiting area, and laid down.

"Have your pick of tables, ladies!" Ebba shouted from the kitchen. "What do you all like to eat?"

"I'm not really hungry," Opaline stated as she pondered why she had let them talk her into coming here.

"You're not going to get out of trying my food that easily. In that case, I'll make you one of my favorites. I can guarantee you're going to love it. Paula, you hungry?"

"Sure am. Where's the coffee machine?"

Opaline sat and listened to them chatter, interrupted only by the sounds of pans clanging and cupboards opening and closing. There was a kind of kindred spirit that lingered in the restaurant. Her mother had taught her to use her sixth sense to know if something was right or wrong. Ebba's restaurant did indeed feel right. Almost like coming home after being gone for a while.

The aromas of food and coffee began to fill the air and mingled with Paula's and Ebba's conversation. There was laughter and giggles. She wondered if this is what it felt like to have girlfriends or people who care about you.

"Here we go. My all-time favorite, grilled ham and cheese with a touch of maple syrup," Ebba said as she laid out three plates.

Opaline looked at Paula, who was holding three cups of coffee, and they laughed.

"Well, it is, just for the record!" Ebba exclaimed.

"My mother used to make them for me all the time." Opaline picked up one of the triangle pieces and took a bite. "Mmm, just like my mom's!"

"I made plenty of coffee. Should I bring some to the police officers?" Paula asked.

"No, sit down and eat first. Grilled cheese is best eaten hot. We can bring the coffee and sandwiches when we are done."

"Good idea. My bro can wait. So, tell me, Opaline. Are you going to go out with him?"

Opaline coughed and almost choked on the bite of food she'd just taken. "He did ask me out."

"Wow! Eamon asked you out? I hope he takes you here to eat. He did say he was going to stop by tomorrow," Ebba stated.

Opaline saw her attempt to hide her smile, and she smirked. The two of them had taken her very somber life and changed it to make it anything but tragic after the break-in. It was as if they were sisters talking about a new boyfriend over a family dinner. It was so surreal and comforting.

"He didn't say where we would be going for dinner. He did mention he wasn't a good cook."

"That is accurate. Eamon burns toast every time he tries to make it. Let me tell you..."

She took little bites and listened to the two of them prattle on about what to do and not do on her date with Eamon. Before she knew it, her plate and theirs were empty.

"I better get those sandwiches made for the officers." Ebba stood and took their empty plates to the kitchen.

Nursing her cold cup of coffee, Opaline realized she was exhausted. The adrenaline high had collapsed, and the caffeine was about to, too. She hid a yawn with her hand and leaned her head back against the booth cushion.

"I'm ready. Just wrapping up the last grilled cheese.

Paula, make sure you have the little packets of cream and sugar."

Opaline opened her eyes. Paula wasn't sitting next to her. Had she fallen asleep? "What can I do?"

"We have it covered. Athena is still sleeping on the front couch. She is welcome here any time after hours." Ebba laughed.

"Thank you for letting her come." She slid out of the booth, and then she picked up sleeping Athena.

The three of them left the restaurant, and her reality of the night slipped back into place. Her business, her home, had been broken into. She frowned as they walked closer to her bookstore. Some of the police cars had left, and a glass repair truck was parked in front of her store. When they reached the yellow tape, they waited.

Eamon was the first one to come and greet them. "Hello, you can come inside. They are almost done with the window. The glass repairman had to order a replacement. It should be here in a couple of days. They will have to go to the Cities to get it."

"We brought coffee and sandwiches." Paula handed him the tray with the coffee.

"Thanks. Opaline, I might need you to come down to the station in the afternoon."

"Just let me know."

"We should be out of here in less than a half hour. I have an officer assigned to be stationed outside until morning."

"Great." Opaline paused and looked around after bypassing the yellow tape. Her nightmare was still here. Her business was in shambles. "Can I go back upstairs yet?"

"Yes. When you come by the office, we can talk about tomorrow night. That is, if you still want to go out for dinner."

Every logical reason pointed to no, but her sixth sense kicked in again. "You're not getting out of buying me dinner that easy."

Athena meowed, and Eamon reached out to pet her. "I'm glad you still want to. I'll see you tomorrow."

"Wrong. Don't you mean this afternoon?" She smiled at his confused look.

He grinned. "Yeah. See ya in a couple of hours." An awkward silence filled the air as he still stood next to her. "Okay, then. I'm going to go take a look around."

Opaline felt a hand on her back and looked over her shoulder. Paula and Ebba were still by her side. "You guys don't have to do this with me."

"Yes, we do. Because Ebba said she was going to sleep over," Paula said.

She ignored the sleep over remark and walked through the store to the stairs that led up to her home. Leading the way up the stairs, she pushed open the door. Athena jumped out of her arms and ran into the bedroom, meowing loudly.

"What's wrong, girl?" She followed her and found her sitting among a mess of papers on the floor. "Oh, my goodness."

Her use of the forbidden word caused Athena to meow more and scratch at the papers. Ebba and Paula had followed her, then halted in the doorway.

"My, my. This won't do. We'll start in here first so you can at least sleep," Ebba said as she righted a picture on the dresser. "Is this your mom?"

Opaline turned and saw Paula picking up some of her clothes and Ebba was holding a picture. "Yes. That was my mother, Nevaeh. She died about four years ago."

"I'm sorry. I was going to tell you she is—was—beautiful. My mother also passed away about four years ago," Ebba stated.

"I didn't know that. I'm sorry for you too."

"I posted it in the Minneapolis Tribune because that's where we had lived until she got sick. I moved here because this is the town she would bring me to for vacations."

"I'm sorry too," Paula said.

The room became quiet. Even Athena had stopped her very vocal meowing and disappeared. Then they began asking her where things went, and soon the room took on an almost-finished look.

The pink canopy, with its glow-in-the-dark butterflies, had been put back in place around her queen-sized bed. Her brown-and-rose-colored quilt now lay on the bed instead of on the floor. Her large dream catcher was also back in place on the wall.

The piles of papers Athena had been sitting on were the last thing to be picked up. The intruder had taken them out—no, had tossed them—from the box she had kept them in.

"That box was my mother's. She said it had special things in it. She never let me look inside it when I was little. The first time I did was after she died. I never found anything special. It just had a couple of pictures and part of an old book."

"That's sad," Paula said.

Opaline walked over to Ebba, who had gone very quiet and was holding a picture she had taken out of the pile.

"Ebba, are you okay?"

She looked at the picture Ebba was holding. It was her mother with two other women. The three women sat on what looked like a park bench, each holding a baby on their lap. Her mother, Nevaeh, was in the middle, a woman with red hair sat to the left, and a woman with jet-black hair was on the right.

"That's my mother on the left. And that's me as a baby on her lap. I have this same photo," Ebba announced.

nine

"No information found."

Damn it! Stupid program.

Eamon checked the Wi-Fi, making sure they hadn't lost the internet network. Seeing that there was still a connection, he hit Enter for a third time.

"No information found."

He was sure the man, Pete, had to be involved in Opaline's break-in.

Crap. He pounded his fist on the desk in frustration. Officer Thomas and Detective Warren turned to look at him.

"What? Why are you eyeing me? Either of you find out anything on a man named Pete from the speed dating event?"

"No," Thomas said. "Does the man have a last name?"

"If I had a last name, I would have given it to you. Just forget it." The question Thomas had asked had been an automatic one. Of course, to do a search on a person, the last name would be very beneficial. He knew that, but he didn't have it. "Get back to work. I want to know something by four thirty."

"But how are we—" Thomas began but stopped when Eamon glared at him.

"Yes, sir," the two men said in unison.

Eamon released a sigh at the sound of their keyboards clicking, hoping it would clear his clear his mind. He reviewed what still needed to be done in the investigation and formed a what-to-do list in his head. First on the list was that everyone at the speed dating event was a suspect and would have to be questioned. Second, why hadn't he asked Opaline for the list of the attendees?

He knew why. He had been so concerned for her safety that he broke the number one investigation rule: don't let your personal feelings get in the way of doing your job.

Since Thomas and Warren had lived their entire lives in Onamia, he was hoping they might have had some previous run-ins with the man whose first name was Pete, and they would be able to find information quicker than he could.

Putting his elbow on the desk, Eamon rested his forehead on his palm. He had very minimal hunches to go on. The only evidence the team had found on site was a screwdriver, which supposedly the delinquent or criminal had used to break the lock on the front door. It had been sent to the Twin Cities for fingerprints and DNA testing, but it would take weeks to get a report.

Detective Warren discovered that one of the bookshelves had hit the glass window, which had caused it to shatter. But they hadn't been able to pull any fingerprints; there were too many on it, and most would probably be customers. The department wouldn't be able to run all of them.

When he had questioned Thomas and Warren about their walk around the building, they had informed him no one had done one. *What a huge mistake,* Eamon thought.

Big city versus small town, detective work was now his problem too. The whole police force was acting as if the break-in was nothing, just some kids pranking The Book Store.

He, on the other hand, had a different point of view. Kids never did that much damage without taking something of value. That was his first observation, that nothing had been taken from the store. Yes, the place had been trashed, but whoever had done it had been looking for something. He was sure of that.

But what? That was among the many unsolved questions he had.

Was it one criminal, or had it been a group? Had they found what they'd been trying to find? Were they going to come back to look again if they hadn't found it?

It. What was *it?*

Damn, he was going down a rabbit hole leading to more questions. Eamon sat back in his chair, stretching his legs under the desk. He allowed his mind to go to the person he had been trying not to think of—Opaline. Even now, he could picture her face and beautiful green eyes. When he found her upstairs unharmed, he had been so relieved.

His eyebrows drew together. What was wrong with him? He barely knew her. They had only just met at the speed dating event, and he was acting as if they were in some sort of relationship.

He checked his watch. She should be arriving soon. What would he say to her? He had no update to give to her.

Picking up his phone, he tapped in the bookstore's number. It rang and rang. Ending the call, he tapped Paula's number.

"Hey, what's up?"

"I'm glad you answered," Eamon stated and then cleared his throat. "Are you with Opaline?"

"No, but I'm heading that way now."

"Good. Opaline didn't answer the store's phone. Can you have her call me?" He heard the clicking sound of Paula's turn signal.

"Do you want her to call you? Or...do you want her to call your office?"

He guessed what her underlying question was. Did he want Opaline to call him, Eamon, so he could hear her voice and know she was all right? Or did he want Opaline to call Detective Dayan?

"It's a bit early for your cheekiness."

Paula laughed. "Every chance I get, bro."

Sighing deeply, he paused before saying, "Just have her call me."

"Gotcha. Call Eamon. Bye."

And then the call ended. *Damn Paula.*

ten

The smell of coffee and food and the sound of pounding made Opaline open her eyes. She lay tightly in a cocoon made of her quilt with Athena snuggled on her loft of pillows by her head. Athena half-opened her eyes, lazily yawned, and winked.

"Okay, Miss Athena, we better get going."

The cat closed her eyes, ignoring her comment.

"Okay, you can have a few more minutes, but that food smells good."

She hadn't been able to disregard the madness from the night as a bad dream. It had been a twisted nightmare mixed with reality.

That moment of Ebba's announcement after looking at the picture kept running through Opaline's head as she tried to drift off to sleep. When she had finally dozed off, weird dreams had invaded her slumber.

Her mother had always made her talk about her dreams when they had frightened her. She had said it was a way to make them go away. Maybe that was why they kept coming to her. And she hadn't had anyone to share them with.

Glancing upward at her dream catcher, she wondered why it hadn't been working lately. It was supposed to catch the dreams before going to the person.

Could dream catchers be overworked? Goodness, no.

Dreams were a good thing, and she reminded herself to light some extra blue candles so they could capture all the negativity and help calm the room.

Pushing off the quilt, Opaline swung her legs over the edge of the bed. Where had the picture of her mother and the other ladies come from? She couldn't remember it being in the box that held her mother's personal things. But then she had only gone through the box quickly a couple of years ago before placing it under her bed. There were too many memories and disappointments inside. She missed her mother every day, every minute, and every hour.

When Ebba had made the startling announcement, she, along with Paula, had sat on the floor trying to solve the puzzle of how their mothers had known each other. When neither of them could, Paula announced it was time to get some sleep and said they were going to have a sleepover. She immediately claimed the couch. Ebba took the guest room, which had been her mother's. They each had said good night and turned off the lights.

It had been odd having someone sleeping in her house but also comforting at the same time. The more she thought about it, she realized she had been lonely.

Opaline smiled when new waves of smells engulfed the room and rubbed the sleep from her eyes. It was a nice reality to wake up to. She grabbed her pink robe from the end of the bed and went to the kitchen.

"Good morning, Ebba." Seeing her in one of her mother's aprons brought forward little sparks of sadness. She inhaled deeply, pushing them away. "I see you found one of my mother's aprons."

"I found it in the drawer. I just love these vintage aprons. I made sure to not get anything on it that would stain. I hoped you were an early riser. I raided your refrigerator. You didn't have much. Tsk, tsk, but I came up with enough stuff to cook us breakfast," Ebba said.

Opaline watched as Ebba turned and smiled at her. "Sorry. I don't go grocery shopping very often. There couldn't have been much to work with in there."

"Hey. Mornin'," Paula announced as she came up the stairs.

"I hear you figured out who was knocking on the door so early," Ebba stated.

"People? Where? In my bookstore?"

"Ya. We let you sleep. We didn't want to wake you. There was a line of people waiting outside who were anxious to help fix your store. So I let them in," Paula said as she sat at the table.

Opaline blinked twice. She knew this couldn't be a dream and pinched herself just to make sure. There were two women...in her kitchen. Her new friends hadn't left, and they were trying to make sure her day started on a good note. "Thank you."

"You'll need to go down and organize the books. I wasn't sure which sections they all belonged to. I'm not much of a reader."

Rubbing her eyes for a second time, Opaline couldn't

believe this was real. It was as if they'd been friends all their lives. Her life was changing quickly. "Okay. First, I want to eat whatever it is that smells so wonderful. My stomach has been growling for the last fifteen minutes."

"Me too, me too. I could smell it all the way downstairs," Paula said and took a napkin.

"It's fresh buttermilk biscuits, and I found some bacon, so I fried some to make another all-time favorite of mine, an almond butter and bacon sandwich with a touch of basil."

"You found all those ingredients in my empty fridge?"

"Yup. It's amazing what you can do when you're limited." Ebba paused and added, "I don't want to ruin the mood, but I've been thinking about the picture. I think I remember the other woman, the third one. She would come to see my mother. I thought she was just a special client."

"A special client?" Opaline and Paula asked at the same time.

"Yeah. My mother, whose name was Olexa by the way, would have several women and a few men come over to our house, and they would sit in her special room. I was never allowed in there, but I snuck in all the time. I think my mom knew, but she never let on that she did. It's weird because the room was very similar to your sitting room in The Book Store. I noticed it last night when I came over."

Opaline stared at Ebba. Her predictable life was being turned upside down. What was going on? "I don't remember ever meeting you or your mother."

"I don't remember you or your mother either, but the room downstairs made me remember coming here when I was little. The car ride had been very long, and it was always late at night. One time, I woke up when she carried me inside. I remember thinking I was seeing some sort of magical place. The lights had made everything in the room shimmer. When my mother saw I had woken up, she told me to go back to sleep and sang a song, which always put me to sleep," Ebba said.

A pounding interrupted their conversation.

"I'll get it. I love being in charge. And by the way, Eamon said to call him," Paula said.

"Oh, that's right. I have to go to the station, but I don't have his number. Sorry, I feel like I'm in a daze."

"Give me your phone," Paula stated, then licked the crumbs off her fingers like a kid before holding out her hand.

Opaline stood and went back into the bedroom to get her phone. "Here you go."

Paula took the phone and entered the number. "I know you had a bad night, but if I know my brother, you are on his radar." She laid the phone on the table. "Okay, girls. On to my next duties."

And just like that, Paula left, leaving her with Ebba. What had she meant when she said she was on Eamon's radar?

"I think your speed dating event might have landed you someone."

Opaline stopped chewing on the last bit of her biscuit and saw Ebba smiling. "What makes you say that?"

"I saw how the two of you were talking and looking at each other. Now, me, on the other hand... I didn't find anyone I would consider asking out. I'm looking for the ever-after kind of man."

"Knights in shining armor aren't real, Ebba."

"Eamon seemed to be one last night. You found one for yourself. I'm sure of it."

Laughing, Opaline stood with her empty plate. "Thanks for the breakfast. It was wonderful. If you're interested, I have a whole section on fairy tales and a section on reality in the store. Maybe I should show them to you."

This made Ebba laugh. "I don't think my ever after is in them. It was no problem cooking. It's what I love to do. I'll clean up and head home. We'll have to talk more about our mothers later. I might find something in my boxes from when I moved here a few years ago."

"Sounds like a plan. I guess I better make my phone call."

"You do that."

Ebba chuckled as Opaline walked to the stairs and closed the door behind her. Her comment had been a loaded one. Ebba knew she and Eamon would be going on a date.

Taking her phone from the table, Opaline went into her bedroom and sat on the edge of the bed. Sliding the bar on the phone, Eamon's contact information came up. She tapped the office number Paula had put in.

"This is Detective Dayan. How can I help you?"

"Eamon—Detective—this is Opaline. Paula said to call you."

"How are you doing?"

"I'm fine. Ebba and Paula stayed the night with me. I'm about to get ready to come see you."

"Thank goodness you haven't left. I don't have any updates, so there is no need for you to come to the police station, but I do have one request."

"Sure. What do you need?"

"Can you forward me the list of the attendees at the speed dating event?"

"Oh, my. Do you think someone there might have broken into my home and business?"

"I can't rule out anyone at this point."

"I understand." Opaline paused and swallowed hard. The reality was that someone was still out there who might want to cause her harm.

"Opaline, are you still there?"

Hearing the anxiety in his tone brought her back to the moment. Did he care for her? How could he so soon after meeting? "I'm here."

"Everything will work itself out. Do you still want to go to dinner tonight?"

"Yes. I told you, you weren't getting out of it that easily. What time?"

"I'll stop over a little before five."

"I'm looking forward to our time together. If you need me, you now have my cell phone number. I'll be downstairs cleaning up the bookstore."

"Sorry that I didn't and don't have any updates, but I should have a lead soon." There was a huge pause before he added, "I will see you soon."

They said goodbye and hung up. She held the phone in the palm of her hand and went over the conversation in her head. It had been odd. More of a personal call than one about the break-in.

Had Paula and Ebba been right? Did Eamon really care about her?

eleven

Alyaaluladonati stood across the street from The Book Store, watching everyone coming and going. When was she going to show her face? The little bitch needed to call the others to come to her. He wanted to go home.

No, he needed to get back to his world.

All of the others would be sorry for sending him to this place. When he regained his powers and took back what was his, he would rule his world and instill fear in them for what they did to him. No one would be safe, and they knew that.

Closing his eyes, he could feel the power inside the building, pulling at him. It was stronger this morning than it had been when he had been searching for the stones last night.

The power was taunting him now.

The mask of a human he was wearing began to dissolve as the streams of energy began to caress him. It was like a drug, forming threads, compelling him to release the diluted power he was saving. He wasn't ready to show his true form to his daughters or this world. They wouldn't be able to comprehend that he was a demi-god.aq

He stepped farther into the shadows of the building to hide from the potency of the power. Opening his eyes, he could still see everyone in front of the store and noted that none of the humans inside had auras of power.

Why was he still feeling the formidable pull?

Suddenly, a woman with red hair came to the front entrance. Her auras were so bright he had to cover his eyes with his hands. The yellow, green, and violet were magnificent.

"Hide the colors so I can see," he murmured.

Removing his hands, he was now able to look upon the woman. Alyaaluladonati smiled and nodded his head. His assumptions had been correct. She was one of the women he thought might be one of his daughters.

Opaline was the beginning of the new set of one. He knew her mother had been Neveah. It always started with the letter O with the three. Then came the one with an N, and last came the one with an E. The first letters of their names always spelled the word ONE.

His daughters' mothers had been Olexa, Neveah, and Eeva. If the mothers had thought it would confuse or trick him by changing the order, it hadn't worked. He had been at this for a long time for their misguided actions to succeed. Putting together the puzzle was the thrill of the hunt for him.

Piecing it together gave him one more of his daughters, the woman with rich auburn hair. She could only belong to one person, Olexa, who had the same color hair. But what name had she given her? It had to be either the *N* or *E*.

Even though his energy forces were diminishing, his sixth sense wasn't. He studied the woman for a moment longer before his spell wore off and he couldn't look at her anymore. Her aura was still blinding.

Cutting his finger with his nail, Alyaaluladonati drew a pentagram on the wall with his blood. It gave him a rush of energy that he needed to do another spell.

"Now that the one is now two, be afraid. To the gods who sent me here, you should be living in fear. I won't shed a tear. I've waited more than a decade."

The words created a time loop, repeating and repeating the spell. The pentagram on the wall glowed and then shimmered. He could see his world, but a rush of flaming blue energy struck the hole. He was pushed to the ground by the sheer force it released.

Someone knew he was making progress and had been prepared for him. Standing, he used the last drips of his blood and ran it over the pentagram. It siphoned the power residue they had used against him. It was so pure, he gasped as it coursed through him and gave him a vigorous boost.

Smiling, he walked away and began planning his return and how to force his third daughter to find her way here to him. This world wouldn't know what hit them when he left, and his world would be hiding in desolation when he returned.

twelve

Athena followed Opaline into the bathroom like she usually did. It was their morning routine ever since she'd been a kitten. For some reason, the cat loved to play with the running water and then lay on the rug in front of the tub to lick herself dry.

"Oh, baby, you can't play in the water today. I'm taking a shower alone."

Meow, meow, meow, meow.

"Sorry, girl." Opaline bent and stroked Athena's head. The cat gave her one of her famous "if that is how you're going to be" stares, then strutted over to the dirty clothes hamper and laid on the closed lid.

Smiling at the performance, Opaline took a box of matches from the shelf and began to light the blue and yellow candles on the countertop. This was a habit she had learned from her mother too, who had lit candles in every room of their home daily.

Within seconds, the scents filled the air. They brought out a comfy feeling and made her think more of her mother. As she undressed, she pushed the sad thoughts away and stepped into the shower with a clearer mind.

The hot water made her skin tingle and refreshed her at the same time. Streams of water cascaded over her face, and she closed her eyes. Wiping at the water on her cheeks and neck, her hand touched the stone in her mother's necklace.

Suddenly, an image of a man's face appeared, but it was too blurry to make out who it was. Was it Eamon? Opaline squeezed her eyes tighter together. Concentrating harder didn't work. The man's face wouldn't come into focus. She was about to give and begin her shower routine when the hazy image of a man reached out to her. He moved closer and closer to her, and not in a friendly way.

"It's time. What is mine will always be mine."

She opened her eyes, stopping the image, and franticly turned around in the small space of the shower. *Who said that?*

The voice had been loud, as if the person was in her bathroom. Remaining motionless, the only sound she heard was the running water as it hit the floor. She exhaled the breath she had been holding, allowing her heart rate to reach a normal level again.

"It's time. What is mine will always be mine."

The words echoed around her again. Using her hand, Opaline wiped at the foggy glass shower door. She didn't see anyone, and Athena was still lying on the hamper undisturbed. On edge and a little frightened, since someone had just broken into her store and home, she finished her shower quickly.

When she stepped out of the shower, she saw the

candles had gone out. Frowning, she didn't understand how or why they had. Opaline shivered.

Athena meowed and sat up, swinging her tail in agitation. *She must have felt something too,* Opaline thought.

Still frazzled, she went into her closet and was thankful that whoever had ransacked her home hadn't torn it apart. It would have taken days—no, months—to straighten out all her clothes and shoes.

She grabbed a simple, pink-colored shirt that had "Best Ever, Love Life" on the front and a faded pair of jeans, then left the closet. Going into her bedroom, she finished drying herself off and dressed.

Athena appeared and climbed up onto the bed. She nestled into the pillows, ready for a nap.

"Okay, girl, behave. I'll leave out your breakfast."

Nothing. No response.

All the noise and unfamiliar people must be getting to Athena too. Opaline kissed the top of her head and went into the kitchen. It still held the smells of breakfast but seemed empty and lonely without her two new friends. Opening a can of cat food, she filled Athena's bowl and set it on the floor.

"Here you go. Your breakfast is waiting," she called.

Still no meow.

"Well, I'll see you later."

Opaline waited for a moment in hopes that Athena would make an appearance, but she didn't. Opening the door, she left and locked it behind her. She walked down the stairs, and before she reached the last step, her stomach heaved a little.

What would she encounter when she opened the door?

With her hand on the knob, she turned it and held her

breath. Voices and pounding greeted her when she stepped through the doorway and pushed aside the curtain. A sense of calm coursed through her. *These are friends, not bad people,* she told herself.

Tears formed in the corners of her eyes, threatening to fall, as she observed the destruction. Her store was a huge mess, but there were about fifteen people moving around. Some were stacking books; others were fixing the demolished bookshelves.

Where had all the lumber come from? And all the paint?

Then, as if someone pushed a pause button, everyone stopped working and turned toward her. For a few seconds, no one said a word or did anything.

"Thank you. Thank you so much. I would have had to close for a long time to fix everything you all are doing," Opaline said as her tears fell.

"Don't do that, Ms. Lunn. It's not a problem. That's what friends do," Mr. Johnsen, the owner of the hardware store, said.

Then she saw Chelsea, one of her customers, working in the romance section. Chelsea smiled. Opaline nodded at her and gave her a half-smile. She then continued to stack more books on the shelves.

Turning a little, she saw more of her customers; Tammy, Leroy, Joan, and even Hank was helping. There were so many of her customers. She hadn't known they'd cared so much about her.

"Opaline, I think the fiction book section is done," Paula said. She paused before continuing. "We didn't have to paint those shelves. How do you want these hardcover books to be set up?"

She took Paula's hand, who squeezed it as she came out of a dazed state. "They can go over on the endcap."

As she took charge of putting her store back together, she realized it didn't give her time to think about how it had become ruined—or about Eamon.

Sorting the books by theme was time efficient, it turned out. She was able to hand off stacks to the people helping, then they put them away.

"Afternoon, everyone. Is there anyone who is hungry? I have sandwiches, chips, and drinks."

Opaline stopped straightening a row of books to look at Ebba in disbelief. Her new friend was at the front door, holding trays of food. After her initial shock disappeared, she wondered how she was going to pay for all that food.

Everyone finished what they were working on and made their way over to the cashier counter, where Ebba was setting out the food. She followed.

"You're so thoughtful, Ebba, but I don't know how I'm going to pay you for all of this," Opaline said in a soft voice.

Ebba put her arm through hers and whispered, "Did I ask you to pay me?"

"No, but—"

"Don't worry. I know all these people too. I'm hoping they will want to come into my restaurant after eating this lunch. It's free publicity for me." Ebba smiled.

"But it has to cost you a lot to do this. The ingredients aren't free."

"I'm getting the name of my business out there to the town folk. If they haven't been to my restaurant, I'm giving them a sampling. Then they might come to visit me in the future, and I might get more catering jobs."

"I hadn't thought of that. Thanks again. I'm going to

make sure I come for lunch twice a week. No, maybe three times."

They laughed, and together, they handed out the lunch plates to everyone. Ebba stayed for a while and then left, saying she had to get ready for the dinner crowd. That reminded Opaline that she needed to get the list of attendees from the speed dating event to Eamon.

Seeing as everyone was getting back to the chores they'd been working on, she headed upstairs to get her laptop. Her computer bag was just inside the door. Instead of taking it down into the store where all the noise was, she made herself comfy on the couch. Pulling out the laptop, she opened it and waited for the speed dating Excel worksheet to come up.

Meow.

"Oh, girl. Did you wake up? Come here." Opaline patted the cushion to her right, and Athena jumped up and nudged her. Opaline rubbed her behind her ears, and the purrs started.

"I've got to work now, so behave."

Athena laid down just as the Excel files opened. She copied the speed dating list to her OneDrive. Then she picked up her phone and began to text Eamon.

OPALINE

Sorry. I forgot to send you the list. Here it is.

She tapped the paperclip, selected the attendee file, and hit Send. Within a minute, her phone rang, and she saw it was Eamon. "Hello?"

"Afternoon, Opaline. I just got your text. Thank you for the file."

"Goodness, no. I'm sorry I forgot to send it earlier. You should have called."

"Paula said you guys were busy putting the store back together. I'll go over it now."

"It's been such a blessing to have great neighbors, and the people in town have been so kind. I would have had to close for several weeks if I had done it on my own."

"Timing is everything."

That was for sure. She hesitated before saying anymore. Just hearing his voice was causing her insides to do flips. "Do you have any leads yet?"

"No, but rest assured we are working on it."

"I heard some of the people talking about a man they saw walking down Main Street last night," Opaline said.

"Tell them to stop by the police station. They can give us a description of the person."

"Right. I should have told them to do that anyway. You missed lunch. Ebba brought over food for everyone."

"I would have loved to have had some lunch. I haven't had anything yet," he stated.

"Do you want me to save some for you?" She hoped he would say yes, because that meant she would get to see him.

"No, that's okay. I have to look over the list you sent. Besides, I don't want to spoil my dinner. I hear Ebba is a wonderful chef."

"I can tell you she is. She made Paula and I an awesome breakfast."

He laughed. "I better get going. If you hear anything more, text or call me."

"I will do that. What time will you be here?"

"I plan on being there by four thirtyish. I want to take

another look around the outside of the building. Then we can talk more."

He was being so nice. His voice calmed her. An image of Eamon in a pair of jeans that hugged his cute butt came to mind. He had a really nice ass. She had gotten a good look at it during the speed dating sessions. Would he be wearing a T-shirt that would've looked—no, that would act—like a second skin on his muscular body? That would be sweet if he did.

Opaline smiled at the thought but knew he would be wearing dress pants and a collared shirt since he was coming from work. "Sounds great. Don't worry. I'm sure Ebba will hold our table if we are late."

"Right. It always pays to know the owner."

They laughed and said goodbye. Just as she ended the call, she heard footsteps, and someone called out.

"Are you up here, Opaline?"

"I am, Paula."

She came into the living room and stopped. "Were you just talking to my bro?"

"Yes. How could you tell?"

"You look a little flushed. Just like you did last night when we talked about him."

"He is very sweet, and I like him. He said he would be over around four thirty. I'm thinking we should have everyone leave about three and call it a day. I'll need some time to get ready for my date." Opaline refused to look at Paula. It felt weird talking to her about her brother.

"I'll handle that. Why don't you stay up here? I'm so excited for you. You are the first girl he has asked out in a long time."

"I'm sure he doesn't tell you about every woman he dates," she said as she stroked Athena's head.

"No, but I've been well-informed. I know you will have fun. By the way, when is your next speed dating event?"

"I was going to have it in two weeks, but now, with my store in shambles, I'm not sure. I'll have to contact Mr. Horton."

"You should stay on schedule. Don't let the culprit make you change things. Don't give them that power."

"You're right. I'm going to have another event in two weeks, and you are going to be my assistant."

"Wow. You want me to help you? I can do that. We can chat about it later. I better get back to stacking."

"Okay. Thanks again for everything," Opaline said.

"That's what friends are for." Paula shrugged her shoulders and walked away, waving.

Leaning back on the couch, Opaline closed her eyes. The stress from seeing her store ruined and the image of the man she'd seen while taking her shower was taking its toll on her. With one hand on Athena and the other wrapped around the stone in her necklace, she fell asleep thinking of her mother.

thirteen

"We are receiving calls about a suspicious male in town last night. No one can give us a description."

"Damn it. Call the other businesses around The One Book Store to see if they have any security cameras. Then get their feeds or footage," Eamon said.

"Not many of the businesses have them," Officer Thomas stated.

"Don't assume anything. Just do it." Eamon shook his head. What didn't these officers get? This was an investigation. These were things they should be doing on their own. Why was he having to micromanage them?

"Sir, we have a disturbance on Main Street. A white male is handing out roses," Officer Warren stated.

Eamon stood and walked over to him. Was he being pranked by his fellow officers? "Why should we be concerned about a man handing out roses? I think the break-in at the bookstore is more important."

"The man is Pete Cline. He is on the list you gave us," Officer Warren stated.

"He was an attendee at the speed dating event? Why didn't you lead off with that?" Eamon demanded as he focused on the computer screen.

"Sorry. Yes, he was, according to the list you got from Miss Lunn."

The face on the screen looked familiar. He began to pace back and forth around the small office. "Does he have any priors?"

"Hold on. I'm running his name through the system as we are talking." There was a pause, and then Warren continued. "What do you know, he does. It's only a citation last year for jaywalking. Other than that, he is clean."

Eamon stopped midstride and retraced his steps to stand behind Warren, allowing him access to the face again. A spark of recognition came to him. The man he was looking at had given Opaline some trouble last night.

"Tell all responding officers to proceed with caution. I'm on my way now to the location."

"Yes, sir. We'll be right behind you."

It was like a comedy affair with Warren and Thomas. They were always saying things in unison. He was pretty sure they weren't doing it on purpose, but it was annoying. He rolled his eyes as he walked back to his desk. Eamon grabbed his suit coat from his chair and Opaline's investigation file.

Getting into his black Chevy Malibu, he threw his suit coat and the file over to the passenger seat. As he drove out of the parking lot, he refrained from using the siren but turned on the police lights. The station was only a few blocks away from Main Street, and there was no need to let everyone know he was coming.

What was with this guy, Pete Cline? Eamon recalled that during one of the breaks, a lady had gotten very upset about Pete. *No,* he corrected his line of thinking. Opaline had said the woman had acted upset, which had confirmed by her actions at the bar. The more he thought about their interaction, Opaline hadn't revealed what had caused the woman to complain.

Making a right turn onto Main Street, he saw the suspect, Pete Cline. He was standing in the middle of the street with an arm full of roses. Traffic had come to a complete stop. Weaving in and out of the stopped cars, he pulled up next to Pete and rolled down the window. "Are those roses for sale?"

Pete halted his twirling in a circle and dropped the roses. He then stood completely still, staring off into nothing.

Eamon shifted the car into park, then opened the driver's side door. "Mr. Cline, do you know where you are?" he asked as he exited.

Pete was now standing with his back to him. With care, Eamon walked around him so he could see his face. The man had a blank stare on his face, and he wasn't blinking. Instinctively, Eamon placed his right hand on his gun, which he had tucked into the back of his belt and used his left hand to touch Pete's shoulder. "Sir, are you all right?"

That did the trick. Pete blinked, and the blank stare was replaced with confusion.

"Sir, are you in need of assistance?"

Pete peered at him. His mouth opened to say something, but no words came.

Keeping his hand on his gun, Eamon gently moved Pete to the sidewalk. However, the street was now becoming a chaotic mess. Warren and Thomas arrived, blocking the intersection from the other sides, and bystanders were inching closer to him.

"Everyone, back away," he yelled.

"Do I know you?" Pete asked.

"Can you tell me your name and why you were in the middle of the street with roses?"

"M-y-y-y-y name-e-e is.... My name is Pete Cline. I'm supposed to give roses to auburn-haired women. Where are my roses?"

The man wasn't showing the normal signs of a drug-induced state. His eyes weren't dilated. He wasn't sweating, but his statement was a lie. The lines that formed on his forehead and around his eyes told Eamon that he wasn't telling the truth.

"Have you been drinking?" This question he could answer as a no too. There was no smell of alcohol on Pete's breath.

"No. I need my roses. Where are they? I have to give them to women with auburn hair as an apology."

With all his training on how to read people, Pete was stumping him. Then he recalled during the speed dating event, walking up to Opaline and touching her shoulder. She had been mumbling something about roses and women.

"Take Mr. Cline into custody," he said, relaxing his grip on his gun as Thomas and Warren joined him. "Make sure they do a full toxicology on him. Run his prints too."

"Eamon, what's going on?"

He stopped midsentence and turned to find his sister and Opaline just beyond the line Warren and Thomas had established. "Please stay back," Eamon said, then turned his attention back to Pete. "Text me if anything comes up."

Warren and Thomas nodded.

"Okay, sir. I will file the reports on this," Warren said.

Thomas took out a pair of handcuffs. "Sir, you have the right to remain silent..."

Eamon stepped back to confront Paula and Opaline. "What are you two doing here?"

"I saw the lights and told Opaline to come with me."

"I was taking a nap... I was resting, and Paula yelled for me to come quickly."

He escorted them away from the crowd. "Paula, you should know better than to chase the lights. I've told you a hundred of times not to."

"Like that has ever stopped me. I know that man from the speed dating event. What did he do?"

Eamon shook his head. His sister was worse than a two-year-old going through the terrible twos. He noted that Opaline looked a little flushed and was holding onto a pendant she was wearing around her neck. "I'll walk you back to the bookstore. I can take your statements there."

"My statement? What did I do? Don't go all detective on me."

"Paula, stop. Opaline, do you remember Mr. Cline from last night?"

"I do," she said and dropped her hand from her necklace. "I was talking to another attendee, Jill. She was trying to warn me about him. And then you came up behind me."

"Right. Something about not wanting to date him."

"Yes, and she was complaining about him. She had gone out on a date with him and . . . This is too embarrassing to finish." Opaline stopped and looked at him.

"It's okay. Nothing you tell me will go beyond this point," he said, taking her hand into his.

Eamon scrutinized the look on her face, and then she met his stare. Everything around them stopped. He couldn't hear voices, the sounds of the car engines, or Paula, whose mouth was moving.

Things around them began to blur. Then he and Opaline were walking among flowers, and the sky was purple and yellow. It was just the two of them. She reached up and placed a hand on his cheek, then leaned in and kissed him.

Sparks of silver and blue lights showered down on them. When they finished their kiss, violet glowing streams were encasing their bodies.

She released his hand, and things went back to normal. Paula was asking a string of questions, and all the sounds came back in full force, and he winced at the loudness.

"Did you—"

"Were we—"

"Will you pay attention to me, Eamon?" Paula demanded as she placed her hands on her hips.

Blinking, he refocused on Opaline, who was frowning at him. "I hear you, Paula, but I'm trying to talk to Opaline and hear what she is afraid to say." He used all his skills to hide his emotions.

Was he having a nervous breakdown? Had he inhaled some drug from being so close to Pete?

Not ruling that out, he took a few steps away from Opaline in case he had some on him.

"Eamon, like I said, this is embarrassing. She—that is, Jill—had said that they had sex, and it had gotten rough. But she had assured me she had consented and that he only liked to date women with auburn hair. I was going to ban him from any future events," Opaline stated. Once again, she was touching her necklace.

"Holy beegeezus. Really. We have a town stalker."

"Paula, this is serious," he said as they came to the store's entrance. Several people were still working inside.

"That's all I know, Eamon."

"Thanks. I'll look into what you said. Now I don't want you to worry. I have things to do before our date tonight. Paula, if you think of anything else that happened at the event with Mr. Cline, text me."

"Sure, bro. I have a showing tonight for the empty space over there." She pointed to the location three doors down.

"Next time, stay away from police business."

His stern words had no effect on Paula. She smiled and guided Opaline back into The One Book Store. Opaline glanced over her shoulder and smiled too.

Not letting go of the weird out-of-body experience, Eamon made a mental note to figure out what had happened as he walked back to his car. Scanning the area for a third time, he didn't see anything out of the ordinary, but he had an odd feeling that someone was watching him. Ebba's restaurant wasn't open yet, but the hardware store had people standing in the doorway. They were still watching what was going on with the police cars. Dismissing the feeling, he was about to get into his car when Warren came over.

"Detective, The Cities called and said they're still

running the fingerprints from The One Book Store break-in. They also recommended we contact the Indian Reservation Police."

"Shit. That's not good. If we have to get the Indian Reservation Police involved, we will need to call for some reinforcements from other agencies. They aren't very easy to work with, and they don't like outsiders asking questions."

"Right. It's not easy to cross that line."

"Keep me informed if you run into any bumps or get any new leads. I'll see ya in the morning," Eamon said and got into his car.

"Right, sir."

Eamon nodded to him and closed the door. Checking his rearview mirror, he once again had that feeling someone was watching him. After not seeing anyone, he shifted the car into drive and headed home. He took a left on Spruce Street North, and he turned into the second driveway. Before turning the car off, he checked the mirrors. The feeling that someone was watching hadn't lessened.

Running his hand over his chin, and then his eyes, he realized he was stressed. It was the only thing that could explain what had happened to him a few minutes ago with Opaline.

Shutting the car off, he got out and headed into the three-bedroom, brick ramble house he was renting. He needed a shower and a beer before he could make sense of it.

fourteen

The ground beneath him shook, taking Alyaaluladonati by surprise. He fell to his knees.

Who had done magic now?

He wasn't ready for more energy surges, but its lingering effect formed a fine mist on his human skin. He closed his eyes as it seeped into him.

It was a welcoming feeling. Rising to his feet, he opened his eyes and, for a moment, he saw his home world again. The yellow and purple energies in the sky were like this world's candy to him.

Sweet and pure.

He smiled, reveling in the light of the world from which he was banished. But its presence only lasted for a millisecond, because just like that, his home world vanished.

What had happened? Who had called upon the forces to open the portals to his world? Seeing his home world twice in a matter of minutes brought on a deep foreboding.

As he retraced his steps, he took up his hiding spot between the buildings facing The One Book Store. Scanning the street from left to right, he saw a man holding roses. His whole body gleamed with silver embers.

Then he knew.

Spells always left a residue from the witch who had cast it, leaving their signature on the person or thing. In this case, the silver meant Opaline would have had to have cast one on the man. But why would she have wasted the power?

Nothing made sense.

Did she not know yet she was a witch with powers?

How could that be? She had cast two spells in twenty-four hours, one on him and the other on the poor soul standing in the middle of the street.

Things weren't happening in order. Maybe their mothers had done more damage than he had imagined. Opaline was gaining strength faster than he had hoped for. If her powers were this strong, there was no telling how soon the others would get theirs. His plan to terminate his banishment of this world was coming to an end and a new beginning at the same time.

Alyaaluladonati remained hidden and watched as the police arrived. Then he saw Opaline and Paula come running out of The One Book Store. They halted next to the officer, who was talking to the man who had dropped the roses he had been holding. All hell broke loose then.

He struggled to reign in his excitement at the chaos before his inner demi-god emerged. Humans were so stupid at times. He'd learned long ago that without the energy that war and lawlessness projected, he became weak. But with his daughter, who was a witch, there was no telling the kind of energy spike he was about to receive.

Then the lights and sparks expelled what he craved. The ground trembled. The air thickened.

Opaline and the officer left this plane for less than a millisecond. He was drawn along as they ascended into his home world.

Alyaaluladonati couldn't believe he was seeing the yellow and purple sky again. Then he noticed, just like the man who'd been holding the flowers, that Opaline and the officer shimmered in a silver glow.

It, they, beckoned him.

Time in his world was different. A millisecond in the human's world was like minutes in his world. With all his strength, he forced his eyes to close, and the temptation to go with them was broken.

If he had stayed longer, someone might have noticed him or his signature of energy. He couldn't allow the other demi-gods to know he was gaining the power he needed to make his return. By shutting the crack in space time, Alyaaluladonati brought Opaline and the officer back to Earth. He continued to study them from afar and put two and two together.

The officer must be Opaline's soulmate. Their combined powers had opened the crack. If these two could do that, he could only dream what the other two and their soulmates would accomplish.

His time in this world was coming to an end. He couldn't help but smile as he walked back to the dwelling he had claimed as his to prepare for his exit from his prison.

fifteen

Flustered by what had happened to her when she had touched Eamon's hand, Opaline couldn't help but shiver. It had been weird. Things had gone blurry, like in a sci-fi movie. All she had been able to see was that Eamon and the air surrounding them had turned colors. She inhaled hard and wrapped her arms around herself. Maybe her sugar level was low, she thought. It could explain what had happened.

"Are you okay? You look a little pale," Paula stated.

"I do?" She freed her hands and brought them to her cheeks. As she touched them, she noted they felt cool, not hot. Not wanting to worry Paula, she said, "I'm good. I had fallen asleep, and you woke me when you yelled up the stairs for me to come down. Everything has gotten so bizarre."

"It has. Eamon is even acting out of the norm. He was really mad at us."

"He was? I thought maybe I was taking him the wrong way." Opaline reached into her pocket and touched the strings. "You don't think him being upset wi-will have an effect on our date, do you?"

"No, he is into you. He hasn't dated anyone in a long time. Tonight will be good for him. And for you, of course." Paula laughed.

As they stepped up to the sidewalk, she couldn't help but see the devastation. "Maybe I should have everyone leave."

"Why? Things are getting done. I can hang around in the bookstore and make a list of things that still need to be completed. Besides, I have a showing next door. You might have a new business neighbor soon. If I can get it rented, it will push me to be the top salesperson in the office," Paula stated.

"You'll rent the location. I was wondering how long it would take before a new business moved in," Opaline said as she untied and tied three new knots into the string.

The sounds of hammering and people talking halted their conversation. She still couldn't believe the kindness of everyone. Who would've thought her customers would come to be her heroes? The people of Onamia sure did come together when someone was in need.

"Hey, Opaline. Was that one of the guys from the speed dating event?"

She turned to see Ebba, who had rushed toward them and was now a little out of breath. "It was."

"I dated him last night at the event. I got undesirable tones from him. Made the hairs on my arms come to attention. I'm glad I didn't take his number," Ebba said.

"It's so strange." Opaline released the string in her pocket that still held knots in it to put an arm through Ebba's and Paula's arms as they entered the store together. "I remember after another attendee had warned me about him, I thought he should give out roses to all the women he had ever been rude too. And then there he was, doing what I had thought he should do in front of my store."

"That is odd," Ebba said and then pointed to the back of the store. "There is the room I was telling you about last night. The one I remembered as a kid."

Paula excused herself when a worker called out to her. Opaline and Ebba walked over to the small cove together.

"This is—was—the room my mother loved to sit in when there were no customers in the store. She called it her relaxation room."

"I love what she called it. I can see it has a comfy vibe to it. Thankfully, it won't take much to put it back together, so it's in its original condition. I'd help you, but I gotta get back to the restaurant for tonight's rush. I'll see you later, right?"

"Yes. Eamon and I will be there." She watched Ebba leave and wondered why she couldn't stop thinking of him every few minutes. It wasn't like she'd never kissed a guy before, but just being near him made her body tingle.

She had to stop this nonsense. They were two grown adults. If tonight's date led them to dating, so be it. All she could do was take each moment by moment. No need to think beyond that for the time being. She pushed all thoughts of Eamon away so she could survey the damage to the little room next to the checkout counter.

It needed to be straightened up too. The couch lay on its side, and the cushions were tossed everywhere. What could the person have been looking for to ruin so much of her store? The police had said the cash register had been untouched. She didn't have a safe. So what was the reason behind the destruction? None of it made sense.

She tugged and lifted the couch into its rightful position and replaced the cushions. Then she fixed the two end tables and set the lamps on them after checking to see if they were broken or not.

Her thoughts began to roam again. Could Paula be right about Eamon? How did she know he was into her?

What would matter if he hadn't been on dates? Sometimes life and careers got in the way. Why was she making excuses for her own attraction to him? Or why was she thinking about starting a relationship when her life was a mess?

For a third time, she pushed thoughts of her and Eamon away. She had a job to do in her store. Trying to refocus on straightening the room, she remembered Ebba had said something about it.

The room had glimmered. How could that have been true?

She couldn't see any hints of anything that sparkled. And she hadn't seen any when she had painted the wall blue a few years ago. As she studied the curtains that doubled as a door, she thought that some of the purple threads might have picked up some of the light. But then she decided she was pushing too hard to see things that just weren't there. Nothing glistened or sparkled. She ran her hands over the curtains and noticed that the backside of the fabric was slightly faded. Her skepticism was confirmed. Nothing in the fabric glittered on either side.

Opaline turned around slowly at first and then faster to see if anything glimmered. The only thing that her peripheral vision had caught was the glass table with its brass base. But it was a dull shine, which was normal with the lights.

What could a child have seen that they would have imagined glimmering? As she looked around, deep in thought, Opaline saw something.

All the different-colored earth stones that she had for sale were scattered on the floor instead of in a basket that should have been on the glass table. Could these be the items? The children did love to play with them.

She bent down and began to return them to the basket, which she had just replaced. They were good sellers for the store. There was the lemon quartz, the pink quartz, the cavelian, the blue quartz, and the crystal quartz. Customers of all ages loved them. They said they called to them.

She would laugh and ask the customers what they said to them. She thought it was a funny comeback, but the customers would give her quirky looks and buy them anyway. After a while, she stopped trying to be funny and would just pack up the stones for the customers.

Once all the stones had been replaced, she sat back on her heels and scanned the room, still holding onto one. She turned it around in the palm of her hand. The light did make it glow a little.

What was wrong with her? It didn't sparkle or glimmer.

"Ms. Lunn, I'm done. Would you like me to come over tomorrow too?" Leroy asked from the archway.

"Sure. That would be great."

"What kind of rock is that? I like how it glows."

Opaline looked at the lemon quartz in her hand. Sure enough, it was. What was going on? It hadn't been glowing a few seconds ago. Shocked, she dropped the stone, and the unusual glowing ceased. Shoving her hands into her pockets, she began to untie the knots that she had put in the string minutes ago.

"Glow? The quartz stones don't do that. It must have been the lights reflecting on it," she said as she tried to cover up the fact that it had been glowing.

"If you say so. I just might have to purchase one of them when you reopen. It was cool," Leroy stated.

"I have plenty." She let out a little laugh before continuing. "Thanks for everything."

"It's nothing. I like coming here. It's my getaway from my life, time. I love the military section you have. It's just not what you see in a store like Barnes & Noble. You have more small-time authors. It's great that you give them exposure. My wife needs me to stop at the grocery store. I'll see you tomorrow."

"See ya tomorrow, Leroy."

She refused to look at the stones in the basket and walked him to the door, very anxious to share the discovery with Ebba later. Everyone else followed Leroy's lead and began to leave, with promises to come back.

Opaline thanked each person. Paula joined everyone leaving and handed her the "to-do list." "It's not long, but I think we might be able to get things completed tomorrow. That is, if the window arrives from The Cities."

"If that happens, I'll be the happiest person alive. Good luck on your showing later."

Paula nodded and left too. Opaline locked the door and took a moment to survey the progress, noting that the store was about halfway back to normal. The newly built and painted bookshelves were drying. Piles of books were stacked next to the empty shelves, ready to be put in their places. The front window was still boarded, but overall, not a bad job for a totally trashed bookstore.

The stacks of books called to her, and she was tempted to work on them, but her thoughts went back to Eamon.

What was with this guy? Why couldn't she stop thinking about him?

Checking her phone for the time, she saw it was almost four. That only gave her half an hour to get ready for her date. She turned off the lights and made her way to the back stairs. As she opened the door, Athena greeted her. She picked her up and snuggled against her soft fur.

"Well, lady, are you ready to help mommy get ready for her date?"

Meow, meow, meow.

"Meow to you too. I see you weren't a good girl today."

Meow.

"I see you found the toilet paper roll again." In her rush to get downstairs when Paula had called up to her, she had forgotten to close the bathroom door. Her bedroom looked like someone had come over and teepeed it.

"You should become an artist. You're always so creative with white stripes." Opaline couldn't help but laugh as Athena jumped down.

Using her phone, she quickly took a picture of the masterpiece before cleaning it up. She folded the string of toilet paper instead of rolling it, then tucked it under the sink, took out a new roll, and put it on the roller.

"Now leave this one alone, young lady," Opaline scolded.

"What? I didn't do anything" is the stare Athena gave her.

It was so typical of Athena, and she smiled.

Now, when she should be thinking of Eamon, all she could think of was the break-in. Who had done this to her? To her store? Why destroy it? What could they have been looking for? It was a blessing nothing had been taken that she had seen.

The questions went unanswered as she lit one of the lavender candles in her bedroom. It didn't take long for the aroma to do its magic by blocking all her worries, her fears, and reservations. The smells did what she needed, and she was able to shift her thoughts to what she should wear on her date.

Jeans might be good; no, they would be too heavy. Maybe a pair of navy dress slacks. No, too business like. She closed her eyes and went over items in her closet.

Her eyes flew open. She had a turquoise-colored dress she'd recently bought. The color would work to brighten up her mood. Besides, she loved turquoise.

Opening her closet door, she went in and found the desired dress, still with tags on it. Just seeing it brought a smile to her face. Would Eamon think she looked lovely in it? It didn't matter at this point; she knew she would.

Before leaving the closet, she took a pair of white-heeled sandals. As she dressed, Athena ignored her the whole time.

"Well, Ms. Athena, what do you think? Will Eamon consider me pretty?"

Opaline twirled around and around. The dress billowed out and floated all around her. She stopped and looked at her hair, which had taken on a wind-blown look.

"I like the hair," she said out loud.

There was still no reaction from Athena other than her

ears turning toward her voice. A feeling of excitement coursed through Opaline. Turning a little to the left and then to the right, she liked how the spaghetti strap and V-neck made her moonstone necklace stand out.

Meow. Meow. Meow.

She glanced down to find Athena at her feet and picked her up.

"Are you surprised I look pretty? I think you are." She gave her a kiss. "I love you, Athena."

In response, Athena licked Opaline's nose and began to purr. She laughed as the sandpaper tongue tickled and scratched her skin.

As she waited for Eamon to arrive, she began to hum a song her mother would sing to her when she was little. "Hush, hush, my precious jewel. Everything will be all right. No more tears. The day will turn bright. The evil will disappear by candlelight. Hush, hush, my precious jewel."

sixteen

After plowing through pages and pages of cold case files, nothing jumped out at Eamon. Warren and Thomas had done several interviews with The One Book Store customers who had stopped in to report they had seen a man walking along Main Street late yesterday. But none could identify the man. The description of a tall, heavily built man who walked with a limp and had been wearing a hoodie could have been anyone.

Was it a dead-end lead?

Eamon shoved the paperwork off to the side and rubbed his eyes. When he opened them, he sat staring at nothing, going over every detail he could remember from the night before in his mind. Something was definitely out of place, but he couldn't put his finger on it or connect the two incidents.

Why had Mr. Cline been acting so bizarrely? He said he *had* to give out roses, not that he *wanted* to. Who had told him he had to do it? And why would Mr. Cline have simply complied?

These were basic questions that no one seemed to be asking. Peering over his shoulder, Eamon saw that Warren and Thomas weren't back from processing Mr. Cline.

He took a yellow sticky and wrote "toxicology report" on it. If there was a new form of drug out there, he wanted to know. On a second yellow sticky, he wrote "gone home" and placed them on Warren's computer screen.

With his briefcase in hand, he made his way to his car. While he drove home, he couldn't help remembering the weird sense of trepidation that had come over him when he had first approached The One Book Store last night. When he had seen the broken front window, he'd had an overpowering urge to find Opaline. Not because it was his job, but because a feeling to protect her had engulfed him. It had come out of nowhere.

As Eamon thought more about it, he questioned why he would have had that kind of a reaction to a woman he had just met a day ago. He hardly knew Opaline. But he had acted like he had been waiting his whole life for her— which he hadn't been.

Then there was the kiss they had shared. It had sent chills throughout his body. He had wanted to kiss her, and when their lips had touched, he had forgotten all his gentlemanly etiquette.

Shit. What was going on with him? He was acting hornier than a teenager. Even now, he wanted to hold Opaline close to his body. He wanted to feel her soft lips on his.

Eamon pushed his sexual thoughts away as he entered his house. As he tossed his briefcase on the kitchen table, he saw the microwave clock flashing the time, 3:32 p.m. He still had an hour before their date.

Quickly, he went to the bathroom and turned on the shower before removing his clothes. Stepping into the stream of hot water, he stood still, with his eyes closed, enjoying the feeling. The steady waves hit his face as he braced his hands against the wall.

The enjoyment of the water was short-lived. Suddenly, his hands weren't touching the wall but a woman's body. His eyes flew open. He no longer saw the shower wall, and the water wasn't hitting him. He was in a building with no roof. His hands were on Opaline's waist, and she was wearing a wedding gown with a long veil.

What the hell is going on? he thought.

His heartbeat pulsated quickly, and a feeling of doom surged through him. Not understanding what was happening, he backed away from Opaline. But she leaned in and kissed him. When their lips touched, a shocking surge of energy consumed him, making him feel invigorated.

Eamon froze and tried to figure out where he was. They were standing next to some sort of an altar. It wasn't like one you saw in a church, he knew that. It was made out of stones.

No, it was bones and skulls that were stacked on top of each other. He had never seen anything like it before. It was like something out of a horror movie.

Opaline's blonde hair began to shimmer like gold, and her green eyes glistened like emerald stones in the daylight. She was beautiful. Her lips were tilted upward in a smile. He should have been afraid, but he saw only love on her features, making his heart ache with love too.

Reality inched its way into his mind, and he blinked, which enabled him to see things more clearly. He was a hundred percent sure that this thing—no, creature—in front of him wasn't really Opaline. Eamon pushed it away from him. Its eyes began to change. Now they twinkled with a mixture of blue and yellow lights.

What did this creature want from him? He tried to ask, but he had no voice. It continued to cling to his hand until a deep darkness encircled them. He forced his eyes to close, trying to block the impenetrable blackness, not wanting her—it—to leave.

"Eamon, where are you? I got you something for tonight."

His eyes sprung open. *Paula?*

He breathed in huge gulps of air while also getting a mouth full of water. Coughing, he spat it out and moved away from the pelting jet streams.

What the hell had just happened? He realized he had never left the shower. Could he have fallen asleep and had a nightmare?

No, that couldn't have happened. He would have fallen to the floor if he had suddenly gone to sleep. As he evaluated the situation, he removed one arm from the wall and then the other. Hot water continued to pelt him as he lifted his left leg and then his right leg.

What the fuck?

He was unable to comprehend what had happened to him or understand the scenes he'd seen. Eamon ran his hand through his wet hair, then wiped the water from his eyes and turned to lean against the shower wall. He stared at nothing as his breathing slowed to a normal pace.

"Hello, Eamon!" Paula called out from the other room.

He gripped the shower curtain as a form of protection upon hearing his sister. He was almost positive Paula wouldn't enter the bathroom, but he wouldn't put it past her to do it. *Damn. How had I forgotten Paula had a key to my house? Why did I give her one in the first place?*

"I'm in the shower!" he yelled. Turning the water off, he exited the shower and toweled off. Draping and tucking the corners of the towel around his hips, he walked out of the bathroom. "What are you doing here?"

She stood in the narrow hallway simply smiling at him. "No need to get angry. Good to see you too. I see you're still as fit as ever."

"Stop stalling. You didn't come here to discuss my six-pack." He crossed his arms over his chest. "Why are you here?"

"Stop being so gruff. I bought you a new outfit to wear tonight. I want you to look—"

"You did what?"

"Did you forget to wipe the water out of your ears? I said I bought you some new clothes."

A smile reached her eyes, and he knew she was hiding the real reason she had come over. Damn sisters. Why did he have to have a meddling one?

Before he could reply, his phone rang, but he let the call go to voicemail. He didn't want to talk to them in front of Paula.

"Why are you really here?"

"Oh, Eamon. Because I love you. When my big brother has a date, which you haven't had in years, I have to look out for you. I've seen your closet. I know you haven't bought anything new in years. So I took it upon myself to make sure you have something to wear." She held out a bag.

"For the love of God, you're incorrigible. First, you drag

me, like a kid, to a speed dating event, and now you buy me clothes. You have to stop, Paula."

"After this date, I will. I like Opaline, by the way. I have a new client who wants to see a business location on Main Street in an hour. I'm leaving. Now take this and go get ready."

Eamon took the bag she held out, nearly dropping his towel.

"Yuck. Thank God I didn't have to see that. It would have left a scar on me forever." She laughed as she turned away. "Got to go. See ya."

He shook his head as she walked out and shut the door. What was he going to do with his outspoken sister? But she was right. He hadn't purchased any new clothes in a long time. There had been no need to.

Taking the bag into his bedroom, he let the towel drop and smirked at the thought of seeing his sister's face if the towel had fallen. It would have served her right for walking in on him.

The fact that this was his first date in months hit him. Was he ready to move on?

He must be or his mind and body were betraying him. It had taken him a while to get over his ex-girlfriend's death. They hadn't been dating long, but it still hurt.

When a person begins to care about someone and that person leaves, of course it's going to affect the person—as it had him. The Minneapolis police had never caught the hit-and-run driver. Her case was still open and haunted him.

His phone buzzed again, but this time it was a text message. Glancing down, he saw it was from Paula. It was simply a smiling emoji with hearts.

He had to hand it to her. She had a way of getting through to him. Almost like a sixth sense. The emoji did the trick, and he pushed the thoughts of Julia away.

In doing so, he noticed the time: 3:47 p.m. Damn, he had to hurry. He didn't have time to think about what had happened in the shower either. Taking the new clothes out of the bag, he took off the tags and put on the jeans and a button-down white shirt. They fit him. He was impressed Paula knew his size.

He slipped on his dress shoes, grabbed his briefcase off the kitchen table, and left. It was only a three-minute drive to Main Street, and he drove to the back parking lot of The One Book Store. He parked next to Opaline's Tahoe.

Man, you got to love a woman who drives a truck, he thought.

Exiting his car with his evidence kit, he walked the length of the parking lot, looking for a sign or signs, anything that might help—a misplaced stone, footprints, or an object. Not seeing what he had hoped to, Eamon turned and proceeded to Opaline's backyard. He stood there, looking at everything. There was a stone bench, some walking stones, and a privacy fence.

Then he saw it. There was something along the edge of the fence. How had his department missed it?

Quickly, he walked to the very back of the yard to the fence. Pulling out a plastic bag and a pair of latex gloves, he scooped up a piece of cloth that was lying in the grass.

Seeing footprints in the dirt, he carefully moved around them, making sure not to disturb them. Slipping his phone out of his pocket, he took several pictures of the footprints. Next, he snapped some of the surrounding area.

With trained eyes, he took a second to look at the

building. As he stood next to the footprints, he saw that the apartment above The One Book Store had a huge picture window. A flash of anger overtook him.

At that moment, he saw Opaline walk through her living room. Anyone from this vantage point could have been watching her comings and goings undetected, night or day, for a period of time.

Is someone stalking her? God damn it.

He tapped the screen on his phone and hit Office.

"Hello. Officer Thomas."

"Thomas, Eamon."

"Yes, sir. What can I do for you?"

"I need someone to get over to The One Book Store. I found some footprints in the dirt and grass. Plus, have a unit start combing the other side of the fence in Miss Lunn's backyard." Eamon paused and stared at the window again. "No need to inform her. I'll do it."

"Yes, sir."

"I have some potential evidence that I picked up. I'll swing by the office later. Keep me abreast of anything else that is found," Eamon stated.

They disconnected, and he walked back to his car, placing the evidence kit in the back seat. As he approached Opaline's back door, he surveyed the area for a third time before pushing the doorbell. Nothing happened, so he knocked. This time, he heard footsteps, and he took a step backward just as the door opened.

"Hi, Eamon," she said as she held the door open. "Did you want to come in, or should we head down to Ebba's place?"

Oh my God, she is beautiful. Absolutely beautiful.

Gone was her perfectly combed hair from yesterday's

event. It now had the appearance of what he would call a just-made-love look. It was sexy. He was tempted to kiss her, but he pulled in the reins on his desire. He was here on business first.

"Yes. Let's walk. We can talk about the break-in. I promise our conversation will only last until we reach the restaurant," he said.

"Okay. I need to go back upstairs and get my purse. I'll be right back."

She turned and walked back up the stairs. Again, he couldn't take his eyes off of her. There was an air of sensuality about her that intrigued him. The dress she was wearing was a tease. The hem danced around her legs, causing a welcoming rush of excitement to run through his veins. Then, like the wind, she disappeared and reappeared in a matter of a minute.

As she walked down the stairs, his gaze left her face and dropped to her bare shoulders. He followed the thin spaghetti straps to the V-neck. The neckline only slightly concealed the swell of her breasts. It was as if they were trying to come out, begging him to touch them. The movement had him shifting unconsciously from hip to hip to ease the aching in his loins.

Slow down.

He wasn't sure why his sexual emotions were in overdrive. Again, he had to force away his thoughts of carrying her back up the stairs to her bedroom.

"Eamon, is there something wrong?"

He cleared his thoughts and looked at her face. It was the wrong move. Without thinking, he gathered her close and kissed her inviting lips. She welcomed him, just like last night. He deepened the kiss, moving his hands from her arms to frame her face.

"Opaline, you are so beautiful," he said when they came up for air.

"Thank you," she murmured and smiled shyly.

"I should apologize for kissing you so abruptly," he said.

"No need. I wouldn't accept it. I wanted you to kiss me. It's all I could think about since last night."

He met her gaze and smiled too. "Then that makes two of us. Before I carry you back up the stairs to make love to you, we better get some fresh air and get to our dinner reservation."

"Is that a promise for later?" Her voice had turned into a silky whisper.

He took a deep breath. Her invitation was what he had been hoping for. "It could be. Just don't tell Paula."

She laughed, and it electrified the air. He felt a warm but cool breeze around them. Like two opposites mixing together.

Satisfied that the night would, or could, end up the best thing that had happened to him in a long time, he held open the door. When she walked by him, her breasts gently brushed against his arm, making him rethink his gentlemanly actions.

seventeen

Opaline rode out the sparks and fought the overwhelming urge to grab Eamon's hand and take him upstairs when her breasts had brushed up against his arm. But then she noticed the silence that had fallen over them as they walked. Taking action, she asked, "What have you found out about the break-in?"

Eamon seemed startled by her question and released her hand. Had he been affected by their accidental intimate touch too?

"Nothing, really. Thanks to your customers and some other business owners, they reported seeing a suspicious man in the area last night. What about you? Do you recall anything out of the ordinary?"

Opaline clasped her hands together in front of her, hoping he couldn't hear her hammering heart. "No. I closed the store on time because I didn't want to be late for the speed dating event. I went upstairs to get ready. I left my home via the back door, the same entrance you came to."

They reached Main Street and went around the corner of her building and walked in front of her store. He paused and looked around. She did too but avoided the boarded-up front window.

What could he be looking for? Everything seemed normal and quiet for a Thursday night. There were only a few people walking the street and cars in parking spots.

"Do you know if the Onamia hardware store has a security camera?"

"Do you mean Mr. Johnsen's hardware store?" Opaline asked and then laughed when he nodded. "Heavens, no. Mr. Johnsen doesn't like modern-day technology. He complains all the time at the town meetings about the Big Guy knowing what everyone does."

"Interesting."

He began to walk again, and she followed as they passed the entrance to her store. She knew she shouldn't be happy with all the tension of the break-in, but for some unknown reason, she was. Just being next to Eamon, walking and having a conversation, wiped away all the negative thoughts and feelings. She felt a warm glow deep inside her. *Is this love?*

"What about the man you received a complaint about at the speed dating event?"

Opaline tilted her head to the side to look up at him. Her heart was dancing with excitement. Yes, she had fallen for this man she had just met. Not ready to share this newsworthy announcement, she refocused on what he had asked. "Do you mean Pete, the guy Jill was complaining about, the one you arrested earlier today?"

"Yes, that man."

Opaline wasn't sure if she liked this detective side of Eamon, as he was very direct and to the point. But then she remembered he had said he would only talk about the break-in until they reached Ebba's restaurant. She inhaled. "He isn't a customer of mine. He's never been in my store as far as I know. I emailed Mr. Horton to let him know about the complaint. I haven't heard back from him."

"Who is Mr. Horton?"

"He owns the speed dating franchise for this area. He hires people to coordinate the events, then gives them a percentage of the profits."

"Someone actually owns a speed dating franchise? I didn't know that was how it worked. Will you give me Mr. Horton's phone number?"

"I would if I could. I don't have it. I've only been in contact with him via email. I was supposed to meet him the other day, but he canceled at the last minute."

"Interesting. I don't think Mr. Cline did the damage to your store. If he was involved somehow, that is another piece to the puzzle. We are looking into that possibility. When you can, send me Mr. Horton's email."

"I will. I'm supposed to have another event in a week. I think I'm going to cancel it."

He stopped and looked at her. "Why would you cancel? According to Paula, the event was a success."

As she gazed at him, she felt a strange, but wonderful, feeling. She could look at him all day and never get tired of seeing his blue eyes. He had touched her heart and soul, but had she touched his?

"Opaline, are you okay?"

She blinked and looked away, not wanting him to see

how she felt yet. "Sorry. My mind wandered for a minute. I just thought, with everything going on, I wouldn't have time to properly host the event. But I really could use the extra cash it could give me."

"I should say sorry to you." Eamon took her hands. "There will be more time to talk about the investigation tomorrow. But I think you should hold another event. Don't be the victim."

"You're right. I will do it."

He released her hands, but she wanted to grab them again. There had been a rippling surge of energy that had coursed through her when he had taken her hands. It had been the same feeling that had happened in the middle of the street earlier today. She never knew love felt this way, with surges of energy that could consume a person.

Instead, she once again clasped her hands together in front of her as they continued walking to the end of the street where Ebba's restaurant, Mignon's Place, was located. They passed by two huge windows with red awnings that faced Main Street before approached the doors. There wasn't a line outside, but when they went in, the reception area was crowded.

"Do you think we'll have to wait long?"

Opaline laughed. "Remember, we know the owner."

"Welcome to Mignon's Place. Do you have a reservation?"

They looked at each other and shrugged their shoulders before turning back to the hostess.

"I don't think so, but—"

"Eamon and Opaline, welcome. Chrissy, these are my special guests tonight. Please seat them in section three-C."

"Ebba, thank you. I forgot to call for a reservation," Eamon said.

"Well, you kind of did. You told me personally that you were coming. I added you to the reservation list." Ebba laughed a little while wiping her hands on her apron. "I have to go back to the kitchen, but I'll stop by later to see ya."

"Thanks, Ebba," Opaline added.

"Please follow me," Chrissy said.

Eamon nodded for her to walk in front of him, and she did, one hundred percent aware he was behind her. The back of the restaurant was different from the front. There were booths with lavender curtains hung on each side, giving the patrons extra privacy should they choose to close them. How had she missed all of this yesterday?

"This is your table. I hope you enjoy dinner with us," Chrissy stated.

Seeing that the table had been set for two and decorated with a vase of yellow roses, Opaline smiled. "It looks lovely. Thank you."

Eamon moved to the side, allowing her to slide in, and then he followed. Chrissy nodded and placed menus in front of them before leaving.

"If you'll excuse me, I'm going to go to the restroom before they take our drink order."

"Sure. I'll wait until you get back." He slid back out, allowing her to leave.

She took her purse and glanced over her shoulder to imprint his face into her memory, as if this was the last time she would see him. The farther she got away from him, the clearer she was able to think. She wasn't even sure why she had said she had to go to the bathroom since she didn't need to go.

What was wrong with her? His closeness was like a drug to her, rousing her to a euphoria of ecstasy. The quivering in her veins lessened when she entered the restroom. If Eamon was her soulmate, wouldn't he have felt it too? What would her mother tell her to do? She clutched the stone in her mother's necklace hoping to get some enlightenment from it. In her mind, Opaline heard her mother sing the same song she had sung while waiting for Eamon.

"Hush, hush, my precious jewel. Everything will be all right. No more tears. The day will turn bright. The evil will disappear by candlelight. Hush, hush, my precious jewel."

But this time, she heard a second verse, one she didn't, or couldn't, recall until now. "Hush, hush, my only strength. It's your time to shine. Pick the flower with care, like I did with mine. You might think it's a dare, but use the stone, the thyme to make it fine. And all will disappear into the air. Hush, hush, my only strength."

eighteen

Eamon watched Opaline leave the table. As he waited for her to return, he fought through some cobwebs in his thinking process. Usually, he was more attuned to everything and everyone around him, but when he was near Opaline, she tended to make him forget things. It was very alarming.

First, there had been the unusual scene in the middle of the street, then the one during his shower, and now this odd feeling he'd had when they had been walking to the restaurant. He had struggled to keep his thoughts from turning to very intimate ones with each step they had taken. He'd had to release her hand to break the electrifying visual thoughts. Even now, as he remembered them, they made him blush. They'd been scenes of them in bed. He had been kissing her breasts while her hands had caressed his butt.

Squeezing his eyes shut, he shook his head to force the thoughts away for a second time. When he opened them and inhaled, the sweet aroma from the yellow roses tickled his nose.

"Sorry about that. Has someone come to take our drink orders?"

The sweet rose scents were replaced by Opaline's lavender perfume. Eamon again slid out, allowing her to get in. Once she was seated, he took his place next to her. "Umm, no. This is the drink menu," he mumbled as he handed it to her.

"Thanks." She took the laminated paper. "Wow, Ebba's gone all out. And this is just the drinks. Have you decided on your entrée yet?" Opaline set aside the drink menu and took the dinner one. "Look at these selections. I know first-hand that whatever she makes will be wonderful."

Her eyebrows and cheek muscles curved, showing him her excitement. He smiled too and decided, before whatever power she had over him took hold again, he had to tell her about his past. Unable to help himself, he took a hold of her hand. "Opaline, I want you to know that I don't go out on dates. I haven't been out with anyone for over six years, but when I saw you last night. I—"

"Welcome to Mignon's Place. May I bring you something to drink?" A male waiter had appeared and was pouring water into the glasses.

Eamon released her hand. "I'm not sure if we have made a decision yet. What would you like, Opaline? Maybe a glass of wine?"

"Sounds perfect."

Lifting the drink menu to see it better, he asked, "Do you have a cabernet?"

"I don't, but I do have a pinot noir," the waiter replied.

"That will do," Eamon stated.

"Thank you. I'll bring it right out."

The waiter left, and Eamon saw Opaline now sat with her hands folded on the table with her eyes downcast. That was a sign she was interested but shy. What had changed in a matter of a few seconds? Had he moved too fast by taking her hand into his? He didn't have to wait long to find out.

"This is all a little awkward, Eamon. I really enjoy being around you. Everything is happening too fast. You make my head spin when you kiss me, but maybe we should get to know each other a little more," Opaline said.

"Do you have psychic abilities? I was thinking the same thing. And yes, all I can think about is when I can kiss you again."

She laughed, and her shoulders relaxed. "Who would have thought a speed dating event could actually bring people together? I'm a believer for sure now. Tell me about being a police officer. I was shocked when I found out you were one."

"Sorry you had to find out the way you did. I've been a police officer for about eight years. My parents' family used to live around here. We would drive through Onamia to visit them. We lived in Edina for most of our lives. Paula became a realtor and began having clients who wanted lake homes. She moved up here, and I followed her about four months ago."

"I wondered what made you move to Onamia. It's not one of those towns that is well-known."

"I'm finding that out. I was ready to get out of the Cities. The cases were getting too messy. It was Paula who saw the posting for a detective here. I checked it out, and I applied. I needed a change of pace. You're stuck with me for a long time. I have no desire to go back."

"You really love your sister. It's plain to see. My mother opened the bookstore when I was little. This is the only place I know as home."

"A true Onamian. I bet there are a lot of you in town." He felt relieved after sharing part of his past with her, but what struck him as odd was that he hadn't been able to read any emotions on Opaline's face. This had never happened to him. It was his job to be able to read people by their facial and body actions. What kind of spell had Opaline cast on him?

"That's cruel," she said and laughed a little before continuing. "Don't get me wrong. I've been to Minneapolis and St Paul. You know that it is a whole different country. My mom didn't like to travel."

"A different country? Really? You are right. Sometimes it felt that way. I've been to almost all of the fifty states."

"A world traveler, I see. I'm teasing you. I just don't like to leave my home. Plus, who would watch Athena?"

"I understand. I might have to take you to the Cities for the annual state fair," Eamon said.

"I have been there. It was one of the things my mother and I did together until she got sick. We went to a slew of doctors, but none could figure out what was wrong with her."

He heard the sadness in the tone of her voice and saw it in her eyes too. "I'm sorry. About your mother, I mean. I know what it's like to lose someone. I lost my girlfriend four years ago to a hit-and-run driver. I—we—were never able to find the driver or the car, which was another reason for leaving the Cities."

"Oh, Eamon. That's really sad. How long had the two of you been together?"

The waiter's arrival saved him from answering the question that always made him tear up. He watched the waiter pour the wine and then informed them the chef was going to be preparing a special entrée for them.

Eamon looked at Opaline, and they smiled at each other.

"Ebba is so sweet. I've never been here to eat before. She brought Paula and I here and fixed us lunch the afternoon after the break-in. I didn't even know who she was until yesterday," Opaline said.

"I speed dated with her."

That was the icebreaker he needed. The conversation took on a new mood. They discussed big towns verses small, books, movies, and even went as far as politics. He found her to be very intelligent. She was book smart about places and things, but that was okay. What would it be like to take her to places she'd never been to?

"I hope you like it," Ebba said.

He and Opaline looked over at Ebba, who was standing in front of the table with two plates.

"What is it? It smells and looks amazing," Eamon said.

"It's my special spiced, pan-seared salmon with roasted potatoes. I added some cinnamon; it makes the salmon taste wonderful. Plus, I baked a honey gingerbread cake with caramel sauce. Bon appétit."

Ebba smiled and set the plates in front of them. Next, she slid into the booth beside Opaline. "I've been so busy today. I told you it would be worth it for me to bring lunch for everyone helping at the store. I got three catering jobs. One is a wedding."

"That's fantastic," Opaline stated. "Can you come and cook breakfast for me every day?"

Ebba laughed. "I don't come cheap."

Eamon couldn't wait to taste the salmon, so he took a bite while the two women talked. As the tender and flaky salmon touched his tongue, a moan escaped, and he closed his eyes.

"I hear the ecstasy in his moans. Eamon must like my favorite dish too," Ebba said.

He opened his eyes and saw she was whispering into Opaline's ear.

"Well, you two enjoy. I better return to the kitchen. You never know what could happen if I'm not there." And then she slid out of the booth, sending them an air-kiss as she left.

"This is amazing, Opaline. Try some." Eamon held out his fork to her. She took the salmon and began chewing it.

"Oh my, it is," she mumbled with a hand in front of her mouth. "Ebba is a very talented cook or, should I say, chef."

"I think we should call her chef."

The dinner went well, and without ordering any dessert, it arrived. They stared at a huge two-layered ginger cake slice.

"Is this a single serving?"

"I think it's a bring-me-home piece." Eamon snickered and stabbed his fork into the dark brown cake.

"We'll have to fight for the leftovers. That is, if there will be any," Opaline said and took a forkful of the cake too.

Eamon smiled and stabbed his fork into it again. Opaline was such a delight. He couldn't believe how quickly the night had gone by. He had felt his phone go off several times and had glanced at it to make sure it wasn't the station. All the texts were from Paula.

She was killing him with being as protective as she was. It was annoying. One of her messages told him to remind her and let her know if he was staying out all night.

Touché, on her part.

Let her know? He didn't have to let her know anything. He was the older sibling.

He didn't even know if things had gone to that level with Opaline. Even if his mind and body were telling him it had, he had to be a gentleman on their first date.

"Eamon, would you like to spend the night?"

He began to choke on his last sip of wine. He looked into the depths of Opaline's green eyes. If love at first sight was real, then it had just hit him. He could see their future together. It was a happy one, and he knew at that moment she was his soulmate.

All of his grieving for Julia had been real, but he realized he hadn't really known her. It was as if a black cloud that had hung over him had been lifted. His heart was hammering in his ears. A tangible bond had been created at the speed dating event, and it wasn't about to be broken.

Ever.

Taking Opaline's hand, he lifted it to his lips and kissed it. "We'll have to see what the night brings. I was taught to be a gentleman on the first date."

"No need to be one since this is like our third date, if you count the two at the speed dating event. I want you.

You have to know that. I just don't go around kissing men like we did. You are an amazing man," Opaline said.

He tried not to act like he was shocked and in disbelief. New beginnings were why he had moved here. "When you tally the dates like that, I only have one question. Shall we walk back to your place?"

"Yes."

It was a simple word, *yes*. It said a lot without having to say any other words that could get mixed up or misconstrued. Not waiting for the waiter to bring the bill, he placed two, hundred-dollar bills on the table.

He slid out and helped Opaline before walking to the entrance. The restaurant had become packed since they had been seated. They were stopped several times as patrons offered their services to Opaline. And commented on how sad it was her place had been vandalized. She was gracious to each one and thanked them. He moved closer to her, to let everyone know she was with him. She was someone to be proud of.

They saw Ebba waving to them from the kitchen window, and together they waved back as they exited.

"Wow, that was interesting," she stated.

"What was?"

"How everyone was coming up to me."

"I thought you knew the people. Or maybe that they were your customers," Eamon said as he helped Opaline put her sweater on.

"No and yes. Some I've seen in town, and some are my customers. It's just odd that everyone is being so kind."

He put his arm around her, and she laid her head on his shoulder. He didn't want the mood to disappear, but his detective side kicked in. "Opaline, I've been thinking.

You should get a security system. I noticed you don't have one."

"I've been planning to get one, but I never seem to find the time. I'll start calling places in the morning."

"Good, I'm glad. Are you always this easy?"

Opaline stopped short, causing him to back step and drop his arm. She stood staring at him with her hands on her hips. It was clearly a sign of anger. "Mr. Dayan! I am not one of those kinds of women."

Eamon's eyebrows shut upward, and his mouth dropped open. Then he saw a smile on her lips and a twinkle in her eyes. "I'm sorry. I didn't mean it in that way. That's not what I meant to say—"

He never finished, because to his surprise, she kissed him. Eamon hesitated for a moment before putting his arms around her. With their second kiss, she took control, and he found he liked that she did.

The streetlight flickered and went out, just as their lips separated and they came up for air.

"Oh boy," he mumbled.

"That, Mr. Dayan, was lesson number one. I'm not all sweet and innocent."

"Oh boy," Eamon repeated. He took a hold of her hand and led her down the street, forcing her to keep up with him. Thankfully, there weren't many people out to see their mad dash. They ran past a woman with black hair.

"Sorry," they said in unison.

The woman smiled as she got out of their way. They were like two teenagers running into the night. They reached her back door, both out of breath. Opaline fumbled for her keys. Eamon took them from her and opened the door. Before it could be opened all the way, he lifted her into his arms and carried her across the threshold, then kicked the door closed with his foot before taking her up the stairs.

"Eamon, put me down. This is silly."

"And here I thought I was being romantic. Paula told me to be romantic." He smiled as they continued upward to the next door.

Her only reply was to place seductive kisses on his neck and ear. She breathed inward and released her breath, causing him to nearly drop her as waves of desire spread through him. *What a temptress.*

"God have mercy on me." He moaned. His words only seemed to push Opaline. She then used her tongue to go over the creases of his ear. He reached the landing and let her slide down his body as she held onto him.

Her dress was bunched up between them. He let his hand touch her exposed thighs. He heard her moan. Taking it as a sign he could continue explorations, he moved his hand to the roundness of her derriere and felt the silkiness of her underwear. She moaned again and threw her head backward. He stopped and pulled back. This was the second time in a matter of hours, and emotions were causing him to lose control.

He pulled down her dress and kissed her lips again.

"Opaline, I want nothing more than for you to let me make love to you, but I think we are going too fast."

"We're both adults. I want you, and I can feel you want me. Why not see what the night has to bring us?"

"If you keep looking at me that way, I won't be able to say no again."

"Good. I'm not going to take no as your answer. Come

on inside. We'll go slow from this point on. I promise not to jump you."

She giggled as she opened the door. He followed her in like a lovesick puppy. If this was what true love felt like, he knew he had never experienced it before. She stood in front of him like a creature from another planet. Was this what his daydream in the shower had been trying to tell him? If it was, he was a lost soul and wished he had stopped at the drugstore for a box of condoms.

nineteen

"Which way to the bedroom?"

Opaline hesitated for a moment before pointing to the right. "You don't have to carry me."

"Isn't this more romantic?"

"It is," she said and found herself powerless to resist, silently telling herself to go with the flow.

When he reached the side of her bed, he stopped. His obvious attempt at being romantic had come to an end. There was something in his manner that shifted, and he was looking at her boldly.

"You can put me down."

And just like that, her feet touched the floor, but he held her against his body. His hands were at her waist, and he was seductively looking at her. She regarded him with her own seductive gaze. His rugged, but handsome, face had her belly doing flip-flops, as she wanted his mouth to take hers. His lips parted, revealing straight white teeth. He was going to claim her mouth.

"Opaline, as much as I want this to happen, I have to tell you I didn't—I don't—have any protection with me."

The declaration teetered on the edge of humorous, but it was very sincere. Her love for him deepened tenfold, and she reached up to frame his face with her hands.

Protection or not, this was going to happen.

Taking charge of the moment, she kissed him. Her lips gently touched his. She pressed them more firmly to his, and they opened slightly, allowing her tongue to explore the recesses of his mouth.

As if he could read her thoughts, his mouth covered hers hungrily, battling her tongue with his. She lost track of his hands until they were tugging the straps of her dress over her shoulders. His lips left hers and began placing kisses on her neck, sending delicious quivers throughout her body. Every time his lips touched her skin, the spot tingled until he found a new area. The trail of fiery kisses ran from her shoulder to the swell of her breasts and had her knees weakening. Besides his arms holding her, the only thing keeping her upright was the edge of the bed.

Meow. Meow.

The very loud sound broke into their ultra-sensual foreplay. Eamon stopped his kisses and lifted his head.

She rested her head on his chest and laughed. "I'm so sorry. Athena can be a handful when her dinner is late. And it's way past dinnertime."

He kissed her forehead. "We'll have plenty of time to ourselves. Take care of what you need to."

"Thanks for understanding. She has a mind of her own." Athena was now weaving in and out of their legs and feet. Opaline stepped back, leaving the sensual cocoon

Eamon had spun in only a matter of a few minutes. She was very conscious of his body as she walked away to the kitchen with Athena in tow. "Sorry, princess. I'll get your dinner."

"The place looks great. You did a lot of work," Eamon said.

She saw he had taken a seat on the couch. "You can thank your sister and Ebba. Without them, I don't know what I would've done. They did a wonderful job of straightening things for me."

Athena meowed loudly, gently reminding Opaline of what she was supposed to be doing. Taking a can of cat food from the pantry, Opaline opened it as Athena jumped from the floor to the counter. She scratched at the placemat under her food plate.

"Baby, what's wrong? I'm getting your dinner."

But Athena meowed again and then stared out toward the living room.

"It's okay. He's not going to hurt you."

Opaline reached out to pet her, but when her hand touched Athena's fur, she received a shock. Her automatic response was to jerk her hand away, and she wondered if the apartment was dry.

Placing spoonful of the wet cat food onto the plate, Opaline took a moment to lean against the wall. Holding a hand to her mouth, she suppressed a sigh and closed her eyes.

Oh my god. I practically jumped him in the stairwell.

Even with a wall separating them, she could feel his desire and was very conscious of his masculine pull. Maybe that was why the air around her was electrified.

Her earlier realization that she loved him took hold. No other man had made her feel the way he was. It was time to enjoy this overwhelming sensation.

He could be her perfect love. Her heart fluttered. "Oh, please let him be as pure as a dove," she murmured.

After she said the words, she wondered if she should become a poet. Smiling and calmer, she straightened, stepped away from the wall, and walked to the pantry and then to the sink to wash the spoon. As she did, she remembered Ebba had whispered to her that she'd added cardamom to the caramel glaze to encourage love.

Silliness. A spice couldn't make you do anything. Or could it? Something was making her feel very, very sexy.

Walking out of the kitchen, she stood in the doorway to her bedroom. From the couch, Eamon looked over his shoulder at her.

"Shall we continue what was so rudely interrupted?"

Eamon stood and walked the sexiest strut she'd ever seen to her. He took her hand and led her to the bed. "If my memory serves me right, I was about to do this."

His hands brushed aside the spaghetti straps, and he placed a couple of fingers along the inside of the neckline. Then he lowered his head and kissed the exposed skin. New spirals of pleasure shot through her. She gasped as his tongue tried to reach her nipple.

A gentle tug from his fingers released her breast from the dress and her bra. She wasn't quite sure if it was more torture to feel the cool air or his mouth taking her hardened nipple into it. He suckled it and used his tongue while his other hand caressed her thighs and moved upward to the warm spot between her legs. The only thing preventing his fingers from reaching her core was her underwear.

Letting her head fall back, she moaned, wanting his fingers to slip inside her. She felt his fingers inch their way inside of her underwear. They caressed her mounds and spread them apart.

She knew she was moist and ready.

And then he pushed two fingers into her.

"Oh, Eamon." She gasped, and her hips rocked against his hand.

"Opaline, I want you," Eamon murmured once he released her nipple and withdrew his fingers.

"I do too." *This is it,* she thought. Her search for love and the perfect soulmate had ended. She had longed for a man to come into her life. Every inch of her body was vibrating to a beat he was creating.

Opaline inhaled sharply and waited for the next verse.

In one fluid motion, Eamon lifted her off her feet and set her on the bed. She laid back, which allowed him to push her dress up. He took a moment to boldly look at Opaline. Her pupils were enlarged, and her eyelids were lowered, all signs she approved and was enjoying what he was doing.

With her nonverbal approval, he tenderly removed her lacy panties and knelt in front of her. She opened her legs, and he kissed the inside of each of her thighs as he moved closer to taking the prize possession.

His mouth captured her mounds. He felt her jerk but held her in place as he suckled and licked each one.

Sounds of her pleasure-filled gasps resonated throughout the room. He used his tongue to find the spot that would give her the most pleasure. She continued to rock her hips. When her hands took hold of his head and hair, he pushed her to the next level until he felt her reach the pinnacles of ecstasy.

Her orgasms were quick. But he tried to make each one last as long as he could before another erupted. As the last one faded, he kissed her inner thighs again and then stood. She looked like a very satisfied cat on the bed.

"Opaline, are you okay?" He felt like a dumbass for saying that. Why he did, he didn't know. New relationships were hard.

"That was... Eamon, come lay next to me." She crawled to the head of the bed, her dress tangled around her waist and legs.

Taking his phone out of his pocket, he laid it on the nightstand, along with his badge. Then he slipped off his belt, letting it fall to the floor, and kicked off his shoes.

Even though he hadn't been sexually satisfied yet, he was okay with that since he hadn't brought any protection with him. He laid down next to her and yanked up the folded quilt from the end of the bed.

They lay facing each other. His blue eyes swept over her face. She lowered her thick, black lashes, hiding her green eyes from him.

"No one has ever done...made me feel...made me come like that before," she said, breaking the silence first. "You fulfilled my every wish. But what about you?"

"Like I told you, I didn't bring any condoms. I'll come better prepared the next time. Let's enjoy this moment." He pulled her close and stroked her hair, listening to her breathing. When it slowed, he knew Opaline had fallen asleep. It was then that Athena joined them on the bed. She curled up next to Opaline's head on a pillow.

"I hope that is a sign you have accepted me too."

The cat didn't make a sound or move. Taking that as a good thing, Eamon kissed Opaline's forehead and closed his eyes too, admitting the truth to himself that he had fallen in love with her. And whatever this sexual magnetism between them was, it was strong, and he liked it.

twenty

"No one dares to challenge the Council of the Gods. You, Alyaaluladonati of the House of the Ancients, are hereby banned from this world forever."

"You do not have the power to do so. My bloodline is that of the Ancients. I am more powerful than you."

"You are right. But your crimes have been foreseen by the Forerunners. They wrote that when your crimes came to be, you would be banished. The Book of Artefacts does not lie. When the moon rises to meet the sun, you will be vanquished from our sight. This is it, so be it."

The crowd that had gathered in the hall cheered. Alyaaluladonati closed his eyes and mumbled, "What you have done will be only a moment in time, and I will find the power to come back."

No one had heard his words over the noise.

The day the moon met the sun, his exile began. They placed him in the human world that he had, and always would, detest. Humans were vile creatures.

Alyaaluladonati opened his eyes and pushed the memory book away. It was his only link to his universe since being banished. He'd been able to hide it in his clothes on his day of death, as he labeled it. The book held a tremendous amount of energy and scenes from before his time.

He had hoped to use it to get back, but he needed witches to help him. They were the only mystical beings on this plane that held power. Over the past several years, none had been able to help him until he had found three that could. But they—Olex, Neavah, and Eeva—had stolen the three precious stones on the cover. Without those stones, the book's power was nearly drained.

Running his hand over the empty spot on the cover, he closed his eyes, hoping to gain insight into their locations. When none came, he exhaled deeply and opened his eyes.

On the anniversary of his existence on Earth, he allowed himself a replay of the worst day of his mortality. He did it to see his home world, but the scene gave him strength to continue his quest to return.

The memory book had started out as a way for him to record his time away from his universe. But recently, it was conversing with him by sending cryptic messages whenever he opened it.

He relished seeing the beauty of the scenes of the palace. However, the others who had scorned him made his blood boil. Placing a hand on his temple, he focused his thoughts.

Why had his home shown itself to him three times in one day? His eyebrows drew together. *What had happened now to have made it possible?*

He had just gotten to his hiding place after his dreadful

exposure in the street, which had given him an insight into his second daughter via her crystal and violet-colored aura. But he'd had to use some of his stored power to keep hidden.

The new daughter had black hair, like Olex.

Using his memories and some of his magic, he wrote in his book.

I am from The House of Ancients. Give me your guidance. I am lost here in this world called Earth.

As his pen inked the last letter, he felt a link to his world. Who was suddenly helping him from the other side?

The energy from the words seeped into him. It had never been this strong.

What if I wrote more?

No! It could be a trap. Was someone on to him? Did they find out the book belonging to the Ancients was missing?

If they were, how could they have figured it out? No one had contacted him in over one hundred and fifty years, and now, in a matter of days, something had changed.

But what?

Taking a chance, he picked up the pen again and wrote in the book.

I am weak. Tell me what the Book of Artefacts predicted. I am innocent. Please help me.

A sudden bolt of electricity spun off the page and hit him on the forehead. He cried out in true pain and squeezed his eyes. To his disbelief, the page with the prophecy appeared in his mind. Quickly, he read it.

It was exactly as the Council of the Gods had said it to

be, that he, Alyaaluladonati, would try to become the supreme god over all.

He forced the page of the book to turn to the next one. After four attempts, it did, and he read.

The god from the Ancients will return to cause chaos within our realm. Only the pure will rule again.

His eyes flew open. He knew it. He would return to his universe and rule all the other gods.

He wasn't a god who took occurrences or circumstances lightly. He liked to ponder different subjects and events for a moment. The more he thought about the phenomena happening, the more he was convinced it was a trick. But what if it wasn't?

Taking up the pen once again, he wrote, *I am humbled by your gift.*

He could play with the best of them. Whoever it was that was suddenly helping him after all these years, he didn't want to piss them off. Closing the book, he slipped it into an empty space on the wall.

"With the sign of the power, I tell you to hide. I am the founder," Alyaaluladonati said.

He hated spells and went with simplicity whenever he could. The space around the book glowed for a moment, and then he couldn't see the book anymore and grinned. The wall in front of him was simply a wall, with no sign of the book.

Before taking the modern device, a laptop, from the table, he checked the windows for signs of the stupid male human who had purchased the land he was hiding on. He'd had to take up a new spot in the attic since the man had decided to fix the rundown farmhouse he'd taken shelter in for years.

Opening the device, he checked his email, another modern-day thing that was so slow it made him laugh. He found adapting to the time around him worked better than using his powers.

Hitting Compose, he typed in Opaline Lunn for her contact information. It then appeared on the To line, and he was ready.

Dear Miss Lunn,

I see from your Excel sheet that you had a successful first event. Congratulations. I will be sending you your first paycheck on Monday. Hopefully, you will honor our agreement of hosting another one in a week or two. The more events you host, the more profit you will make. Again, I apologize for canceling our in-person meeting, I will email you when I have a time slot open again. In closing, remember we are here to make lifelong relationships.

Sincerely, Mr. Horton.

He smirked as he typed in the name. It was his disguise in this world. Soon, his three daughters would know who he was and what he needed them for.

Tapping Send, he waited.

twenty-one

"We are family. I have all my sisters with me. We are family."

Eamon forced his eyes open. That ringtone was the one he had programmed for his sister.

Disorientated for a moment, he lay still and realized this wasn't his bed and there was an arm draped over his chest. Turning his head, he saw Opaline next to him and he remembered.

They had gone to dinner. And after, she had invited him up to her home.

He smiled, remembering what happened. Being near her was suffocating and exhilarating at the same time. The way he was feeling confirmed his earlier assumption that she was his soulmate.

But then he frowned. What had he done?

Spending the night at a woman's home on the first date was a big no. But, as Opaline had reminded him, this had been their third date. And they really hadn't had sex, just some foreplay.

His phone dinged, signaling he had a message.

Crap.

He inched himself out of Opaline's embrace and got to his feet. She was still wearing the sundress, but now the neckline exposed one of her breasts, and the quilt hid her lower half and legs. Maybe he should stay and finish what they started last night.

Nope! The reason they hadn't finished what they had started was because he'd been a dumbass and had forgotten condoms. Reigning in his desire to crawl back into bed with her, he grabbed his gun, tucking it into its holster in the back of his pants. Then he took his badge and keys from the side table and slid them into his pocket before picking up his shoes.

He couldn't resist glancing over his shoulder. Opaline was still asleep, looking more beautiful than last night.

"We are family. I have all my sisters with me. We are family."

Damn. He quickly switched his phone to silence and tiptoed out of the bedroom.

What could Paula want so badly this early in the morning?

As he opened the door, he paused to listen for a sign that he had woken Opaline. Not hearing any sounds, he walked out the back door and proceeded down the stairs. Once he reached his car and started it, he took out his phone and tapped Paula's name.

"It's about time. I thought I might have to wake the two of you up before everyone arrives," Paula said.

Her giggling struck him the wrong way. It wasn't any of her business if he stayed the night at a woman's house. Again, she was being overly protective. Putting the car into drive while the call switched to hands-free, he drove out of the back parking lot. As he made a left turn onto Main Street, he saw Paula standing in front of The One Book Store, waving.

"Mind your own business, sis. And for the record, we didn't have sex. Now take that and shove it where the sun doesn't shine. Bye."

He hit the End Call button on the dash and saw Paula doubled over in laughter from the rearview mirror.

Damn brat. She is the one who needs to find a man.

The clock in the car showed him he had twenty minutes to make it to the office or go home and be late. Making a quick decision, he chose home. It would be in his best interest to take a quick shower and change clothes.

"Bad Boys. Bad Boys. Whatcha gonna do?"

Shit. Now what?

He tapped Accept on the dash. "Detective Dayan."

"Sir, when will you be bringing the item you found at The One Book Store?"

Looking over his shoulder, he saw the test kit sitting on the seat. "I'm running late. I'll have it there in about forty-five minutes."

"Okay, we will be here."

Eamon tapped End Call on the screen.

What the fuck?

He had a job to do, and here he was forgetting about an important piece of potential evidence. He had to get his priorities in order and stop thinking like a love-crazed male.

When he pulled into his driveway, he made a mental note to stop by the drugstore for condoms. Lovesick or not, he was going to be prepared for the next time.

twenty-two

Opaline stretched and yawned after hearing Athena meow. Sitting up, she didn't see any sign of Eamon.

Where is he? Did he go to the bathroom?

"Eamon?" Not hearing a reply, she tugged off her sundress and bra and walked through her condo naked. The fire he had stroked inside her last night needed to be refueled. "Eamon?"

The thought of morning sex filled her with a surge of excitement. Her search for him came up empty. Feeling disappointed that he had simply left without waking her up, she went back to the bedroom.

Meow. Meow.

"Good morning, Athena. I know. He left. I'll feed you in a minute."

She walked into her bathroom and turned on the shower, but there was a knock at her door.

Eamon.

He'd come back. Maybe he went to get condoms.

Looking into the mirror, she fluffed up her hair and patted her cheeks. Almost running to the door, still naked in anticipation, she slowed her steps, not wanting to appear too eager.

He was going to be surprised when he saw her naked and ready to finish what they had started last night. She turned the knob and opened the door. "Eamon, I'm..."

"Shit! Ugh. This is so wrong. I will never be able to unsee that," Paula said.

"Oh my god," Opaline uttered and slammed the door shut. "Give me five minutes."

Paula's laughter drifted inside as she ran to the bathroom and shut off the shower. Grabbing her robe, she slipped it on. She couldn't help but smile too. Her embarrassment was on the verge of humiliation. She wasn't sure how the two differed but knew that no matter how long she stayed in the bathroom, it wasn't going to alleviate the feelings.

Seeing that her face was still flushed, she tied the sash of her robe. Then, with as much dignity as she could muster up, she threw her shoulders back and left the safety of the bathroom.

Opaline opened the front door for a second time. Paula stood there holding bags and smiling. "Come on in."

"Good morning. I brought breakfast. I can... I thought it would be a good idea to come over this morning. I waited for Eamon to leave before coming up. Don't look so worried. I think it's great. The two of you. But clearly—"

"I wasn't expecting you." Opaline shook her head, wishing she could run and hide. It had been very clear who she had thought would be on the other side of the door. "Let's never bring it up again."

"I agree."

Opaline pulled the collar of her robe more securely over her chest. "You brought donuts?"

"I did. From the bakery. And a gallon of orange juice. Ebba is on her way over too. A few people have arrived to finish the cleanup again."

It was clear Paula knew her brother had spent the night. She met Paula's gaze. They then began to laugh controllably as they leaned against the kitchen counter.

"Knock, knock. Hello, what is going on? I could hear your laughter all the way down the stairs. Is this a party?"

"Oh, goodness. I do believe it has turned into one," Opaline muttered in between fits of laughing.

Paula was of no use. She was laughing even harder and wiping tears from her eyes.

What the heck was going on? Her life had been so lonely until three days ago. Now she had people coming and going at all hours. It was so not like her.

"Okay, you two. Get yourselves together. What is so damn funny?"

"I might as well tell you." Opaline picked out a donut. "As you know, Eamon and I had a date last night. And by the way, dinner was awesome. We came back to my place. He stayed the night." She then took a bite of the donut so she didn't have to say anything else.

"That's not all," Paula stated.

Opaline turned to stare at Paula and shook her head.

"Someone better tell me, or I'm taking my egg and cheese biscuits back to the restaurant," Ebba said.

"Fine," she muttered as she poured herself some orange juice into a glass. "To my horrible bad judgment, I answered the door naked thinking it was Eamon coming back."

"What!" Ebba set the box she was holding onto the kitchen counter. "Just who was at the door and saw you in your birthday suit?"

Paula raised her hand.

"Blessed it be. Opaline, what were you thinking?"

"It was a good plan when I did it. Now I see I'll have to be more careful or install one of those looking spyholes in the door." She took another bite of the donut, still not comprehending the scene unfolding in front of her.

"This is wonderful," Ebba stated. "Yup. Knew it would work. The cardamom and the basil I used when I made your dinners last night did what it was supposed to do. I think I need to change the name of my restaurant to the Love Shack."

Opaline almost choked on the donut. She coughed and coughed. "What do you mean, it worked? Did you drug us?"

"Really? Drug you? No." Ebba paused for a moment. "I used spices to enhance your connection to each other, connections that are very clear to everyone around you and Eamon. The two of you are meant for each other."

"I would call that drugging," she said.

The room became quiet. Had the spices made her react to Eamon like she had, and it hadn't been her true feelings? No, it couldn't have, because that had been last night, and she still wanted him. "Maybe it only enhanced our feelings for each other. Eamon is so wonderful. He made me feel things I never thought possible. And he was very much a gentleman."

"My bro, a gentleman?"

"Yes. I can't believe I'm about to share with you two what happened—"

"I knew it! I know a sexually satisfied woman when I see one!" Ebba giggled.

Opaline's eyes widened. This whole girlfriend-thing was new to her, and she didn't know how to act. Should she share with them how she had felt when Eamon had kissed her, tell them that the Earth had stopped moving? Or that she had almost attacked him in the stairway wanting him to make love to her, right there? "But we didn't... I did... was, but we didn't have sex. He didn't have any condoms."

"Oh, good lord!" Paula shouted.

"That's why I answered the door nude. I thought he had gone out to get some so we could this morning."

She watched as Paula and Ebba started laughing. The sound was contagious, and she couldn't help but join in with them. The whole situation was humorous, not humiliating as she had thought.

When the three of them calmed down, Ebba promised to make her something special again for takeout for tonight. Paula changed the topic to the work being done downstairs in her store.

Taking the lead from them, she dropped the Eamon episode too. "What's on the agenda for today?"

"I came over to help fix your sitting area. I went through some of my mother's things last night to see if I could find any picture of us too," Ebba said.

"I'm here for support," Paula stated and shoved a biscuit into her mouth.

"Okay, then. I need to take a shower and make some

phone calls. Top on my list is the insurance company, then my book suppliers and Mr. Horton."

Athena chose that moment to say she wanted her breakfast too.

"If you will excuse me, I'm going to go down and start in on the sitting area. Come down when you're ready," Ebba said.

"Yeah, I'm going too. I'm the supervisor. I'm sure someone needs to be supervised."

And just like that, Opaline was alone with Athena and her thoughts.

Her very short relationship with Eamon had crossed over into the forever for her. She loved him. She knew that with every fiber of her being. He was her soulmate, but he was a police officer and put his life on the line every day. What if something happened to him?

Did he love her too?

Not wanting to think about losing someone again, she knew there was no room in her life for second-guessing. A driving force struck her. She had to take the leap and tell him.

twenty-three

"Officer Warren, I have the evidence I picked up last night. Was anything found when you conducted the search?" Eamon held out the bag with the material he had found by the fence.

"Good morning to you too. We made imprints of the footprints and logged them as evidence. We swiped the fence for fingerprints, but it came up empty, which we found very odd. Our search beyond the fence didn't come up with anything new either."

"Goddamn it. I was so sure we would get a lead," Eamon said as Warren took the bag. "This better give us the break we need in the case."

"Mr. Cline is being released this afternoon. He is showing no effects of whatever he had taken and has no memory of what he did. The therapist said his mental cognit is fine."

Eamon picked up Mr. Cline's file from Warren's desk. He flipped through it. There wasn't much to go on inside. "I'll talk to Ms. Lunn about getting a protection order. Also, keep up the surveillance on The One Book Store."

"I'll take the first shift tonight," Officer Warren said.

Taking a breath, Eamon knew he had to tell him he was dating Opaline. "For the record, I'm seeing-dating Ms. Lunn. You will see my car there tonight."

"Should I put you on the list as a potential suspect too?"

"No jokes. Ms. Lunn and I met at the speed dating event."

"Good Lord, man. Why would you have to go to that thing for a date?"

Eamon smirked. Why? Because his damn sister had talked him into it. "Let's keep my personal life out of this. How is the list of attendees checking out? Any leads?"

"If the attendees were at the event, how could they have done it, sir?"

"There were two sessions. Some left after the first one. That is why everyone on the list needs to be called and verified," Eamon said.

"Now I get it. I'll start making the calls."

Putting Mr. Cline's file back on Warren's desk, he went to his office. Just as he sat, his office phone rang. "Hello."

"Detective Dayan, I received a trespassing call this morning. I know that's not typically your responsibility, but I thought I would give you the chance to respond to it first," Officer Thomas said.

"What's so unusual about this call?"

"The person who called in is on the list of attendees."

"Very interesting. Give me the address and I'll go check it out," Eamon said. After writing the address down, he stood and put on his gun holster. He checked his gun, making sure he had bullets and the safety was on, then secured it in the holster. As he walked out of his office, he slipped on his suit coat.

"I'm heading out to Mr. Waters' place. I'll call if I need backup."

"Yes, sir," Officer Warren said.

Hurrying out to his car, Eamon put the address into the computer, 505 Main Street. Even though he knew where it was, it was a log for the department to track him. He pulled out of the police station parking lot and headed down Main Street. He passed by Ebba's restaurant and then Opaline's bookstore.

About a mile down the road, he saw the mailbox with the number on it and turned into the driveway. He drove slowly down the gravel road and saw a trailer and house that needed repairs. Next to the trailer was a white truck. Pulling up alongside it, he parked.

He sat for a few minutes, taking in his surroundings. Whomever Mr. Waters was, he was definitely doing work on the house. Tools, wood two-by-fours, and sheetrock were lined up, ready to install.

Leaving his car, he walked over to the trailer and knocked. No one came. He knocked again. "Hello?"

"Can I help you?"

Eamon breathed in hard. How had someone gotten the slip on him? What if he'd been shot—or worse, killed? He hadn't told Opaline he loved her yet. Even now, thinking he might not see her again, he felt an extraordinary void inside him. An emptiness filled him, and he knew he had to tell her.

He pushed all thoughts of Opaline away. He had to concentrate on the situation. Slowly, Eamon turned, with his hand ready to pull his gun. He knew better than to leave his back exposed. "Hi, I'm Detective Dayan. You called about some trespassers."

"Right. Thanks for coming. I was—sorry, I'm Owin, Owin Waters." The man wiped his hand on his jeans and then held it out to him. It looked like he'd been sanding something, he had white dust all over himself. He stood about six feet tall and was wearing a baseball cap and a camouflage print bandanna around his neck. Military?

Reaching out, he shook Owin's hand. "Did I interrupt something?"

"No, not really. I needed a break. I'm not the handyman I thought I was." Owin laughed. "I called because last night when I got home from work—I'm a UPS driver—I noticed a light on in the house. You see, I just bought the place as a fixer-upper. When I went in to check on it, I found food and some other things that weren't mine. Would you like to take a closer look?" Owin began to walk toward the front door.

Eamon followed, checking the area. "About what time was this?"

"Around eightish. Hey, you look familiar. Did I see you at the speed dating event the other night?"

Eamon stopped. What the hell? Did everyone in this small town attend the event? "I was there."

"Cool. I wasn't chosen for the second session. But I did find it interesting." Owin held open the door. "Come inside. It's a mess."

"How long have you been living in the trailer?"

"About six weeks. I sold my place in St. Cloud and bought this place and the trailer. I might have to spend the winter in it, which wasn't part of my plan. This house needs a lot of work."

Stepping inside, he smelled the dust and covered his mouth as he began to cough. If there had been any footprints or fingerprints, they'd be ruined now. The place definitely needed a makeover. "You have your work cut out for yourself, that's for sure. Do you lock the doors?"

"I do. I have equipment in here, but the windows are useless. I can't replace them yet. I laugh when I lock the doors." Owin walked over to the window and yanked the shade up.

All someone would need to do is throw a brick through it and they'd be able to get inside with no problem. Eamon's eyes began to sting from the dust, and he fought the urge to wipe at them. "What about security cameras?"

"I have one. It's by the trailer. But now that you're asking, I think I'm going to go buy some more. Maybe even some motion detector lights."

"That is a very good idea. Was there anything missing? Do you think they came in through the front door or the back?"

"I believe the person came in through the back door. I'll show you. Come this way."

Eamon followed Owin through the front of the house to the kitchen. The back door was about as good as the front one. A person wouldn't need much to jimmy the lock or take a crowbar to it.

"When I came in last night, the door was open, and I know I had it locked. Then I saw the bags of food on the counter. I know they weren't mine because I don't eat that stuff. I'm more of a fruit-and-veggie-snack-type guy."

"You said you left the event after the first session."

"I did. At first, I was bummed no one had chosen me, but it was good. Being a workday, I had to get up early on Thursday. I was in bed before ten."

"I'm not much of a handyman myself. Do you happen to have any footage from Wednesday night, confirming when you got home? The local bookstore was broken into while the owner was hosting the speed dating event." Trying to keep the conversation on task, Eamon took out his notepad. This was old school, but he liked it better than recording the conversation on his phone.

"Wow. I can pull it up on the app. Could the same person, or persons, have come here to hide out?"

"I can't rule anything out." Eamon walked around the kitchen, looking for anything else he saw out of the ordinary. It was clear to him Owin had nothing to do with Opaline's break-in, but he had to account for everyone who had attended the event.

"Here it is," Owin stated and held out his phone.

They watched the recording of Owin parking his truck and going into the trailer with the time stamp of 9:22 p.m.

"Thanks. As we discussed, you should get some more cameras and motion detection lights. If you see or hear anything, give me or the station a call. Here is my card." Eamon reached into his pocket and withdrew his business card. When Owin took it, their fingertips touched and a tiny spark of electricity zapped them, causing them to pull away. The card fell to the floor.

"What was that?"

"That was very strange." Eamon bent down, retrieving the card. "Must have been some static electricity in the room."

"Very odd. I'm running an extension cord from the

trailer to here. The house doesn't have any working electricity yet. That's on my to-do list too."

"Mr. Waters, thanks for your time. I'll write up a report to have on file in case you have a visitor again. By the way, I have a sister you might like to meet. She is single."

Owin laughed. "Thanks, but no thanks. The dating event gave me the courage to ask out a lady I've been thinking about. She and I have a date tonight as a matter of fact. We're going to that restaurant on Main Street, Mignon's Place."

"Great food. Went there last night. Tell the hostess Detective Dayan sent you. It might give you brownie points with the chef."

"For real? Sounds like a plan. Thanks again for coming out. I wasn't sure if anyone would show up after I called in. They made it sound like it wasn't a priority."

"Thanks for letting me know that. Every call that comes in is a priority. If you don't mind, I'd like to walk around the house before I leave."

"Of course," Owin stated and put the business card in his back pocket.

Eamon took his leave and walked the perimeter of the old house. The back faced an open field. Anyone could be hiding out there. Taking a couple of pictures with his phone, he continued to the side of the house facing the trailer and took more pictures. Back in front, he got into his car and headed back to town.

twenty-four

After feeding Athena and taking a shower, Opaline pulled out a summer short-sleeve dress and dressed. Then she dug out her mother's box from under the bed. She couldn't stop thinking about Ebba and the sitting room in the store.

Setting the box on the bed had her remembering what Eamon and she had done on it.

Or almost done.

He hadn't texted or called since he had left without saying goodbye. But she reminded herself he was a busy man on the police force. Refocusing on the items inside the box, she began taking them out and laying them on the bed in piles.

Papers. Newspaper articles. Pictures.

And a hand-drawn sketch of a man.

Could this be her father? Her mother never spoke of him. The one time she did was just before she died. She recalled it being an awkward conversation, as if her mother couldn't bring herself to do it. Her mother had said that if he showed up to call the police and not to talk to him. She'd agreed only to calm her mother, who had become very upset.

And that was the extent of her knowledge of her father. She didn't know his name or what he looked like. Unless the man in the sketch was him.

Turning it over, she saw her mother's very distinctive handwriting on the back. It was dated the same year she was born.

"This is the beast, whom I kissed. We hid in the broom closet until it was time to celebrate. Goodness within, Neveah," Opaline read.

Wow, that is deep.

Not understanding what it meant, she set it aside to show Ebba. Her phone dinged, signaling she had a message.

PAULA

We have questions.

It was from Paula. She'd been so lost in going through the box, she'd forgotten everyone was downstairs. She left everything as is, except the sketch, which she took with her.

"Athena, I'm leaving. Have a fun-filled day."

Out of nowhere, Athena jumped on the bed and meowed, pawing at the paper she held.

"Stop. You'll ruin it. Now be a good girl."

Athena meowed and laid on the things from the box, almost in a protective manner.

She left and went down the front stairs. Again, the sounds of people chatting and pounding greeted her.

"Oh, good. You came. I was about to come up to get you," Paula said.

"Sorry I took so long." Being humbled by Paula seeing her nude earlier still lingered, but she acted as if it had never happened. She went over the list of Paula's concerns and the jobs still needing to be done. After a few minutes of instructions, Paula set out on new missions.

The store was almost completely put back together. It was amazing what could be done with the help of friends and neighbors. Not seeing anyone who needed her attention, she went in search of Ebba. She found her in the sitting room. It, too, was back to normal, as if no one had destroyed it. Ebba was on the couch holding one of the stones from the basket.

"It looks lovely. You did a great job. Sorry I wasn't here to help you."

"Thanks. It was fun. My feelings of having been here were true. Look here on the table."

Opaline walked over to the table and looked at the spot Ebba was pointing at. Etched into the glass were the letters *E* and *M*.

No way.

They were so small she'd never noticed them before or had simply thought that they had been scratches on the glass top. "I don't believe it."

"It's real. I know I've been here before. I can also remember playing with the stones with two other girls," Ebba announced.

"How could that be possible? If I was one of those girls, why can't I remember you?"

"That is the mystery we will have to solve. It is like a scavenger hunt. We'll have to have a girls' night, but not on the weekends. The restaurant is too busy for me to stay out late."

Opaline sat next to Ebba on the couch. First, there was the picture of her mother with two other ladies. And one was Ebba's mother. And now Ebba's initials were on a table in her store. Were there more connections?

"Goodness, I almost forgot. The reason I was late was because I went through some of my mother's things. Look what I found." She held out the sketch of the man.

Ebba took it and frowned. "This was in your mother's things?"

"Yeah. Why? Do you know him?"

Ebba closed her eyes and touched the stone in the necklace she was wearing. Her actions were just like what she did when she needed to calm herself. "That is my father. I have the same sketch of him."

"No freakin' way!" Opaline shouted. Then she covered her mouth with her hand. "Sorry, but this is so weird. Why would my mother have a sketch of your father? Look at the back. Does yours have this too?" Opaline turned the paper over.

Ebba quickly placed her hand on it. "Yes. My mother told me it was to protect me."

"What? This little poem is supposed to protect you . . . us? From what or whom?"

Abruptly standing, Ebba looked around. "I'm getting some bad vibes. I'm sorry. I have to go, Opaline."

Before she could stop her, Ebba was walking away. "Ebba, come back."

It didn't do any good, Ebba ignored her and left the store. What had she done to her friend?

Everyone in the store had turned to look at her.

Shaking her head, she closed her eyes and turned away from them. After a moment, Opaline followed Ebba outside but saw she was almost at her restaurant.

Turning in the opposite direction, she walked to the corner of Main Street. Opaline couldn't help but think about her mother. If Ebba and her mother had a connection, why hadn't she told her? She'd tried and tried to remember ever seeing Ebba or her mother in the store or anywhere but couldn't. Even Ebba had said she couldn't remember ever have being together but kept coming up blank—nothing.

Why would her mother have a sketch of Ebba's father in her things and not one of her father?

Just like Ebba had done in the sitting room, she reached for the stone in her necklace and held it.

Who was her father? Should she know who he was? Did she look like him? Why hadn't her mother ever spoken of him?

Releasing the stone, she shoved her hand into her pocket and played with the strings that were always with her. One-handed, she tied knots into it, then she stopped at the corner and waited for the streetlight to turn green. It wasn't like she had to wait. There were no cars coming. Just as she crossed the street, her phone buzzed. Taking it out of her pocket, she saw it was Eamon.

"Hello?"

"Hi, Opaline. Can you talk?"

"I'm out walking. I needed some fresh air. What's up?"

"First, I wanted to apologize for leaving you this morning. But I thought it best."

"I thought you had gone to get something so we could finish what we started."

Eamon cleared his throat. "Right. Sorry about that too. I'll be better prepared from now on."

"Ebba said she would make us a couple of dinners tonight for takeout. That is if you want to come over," she said. Not hearing anything, she looked at the phone to see if the call had been dropped. "Eamon? Eamon, did I lose you?"

"No, I'm right here."

She turned and found him in his car. He had pulled up next to her. "Oh goodness."

He got out of his car, and she slipped her phone into her pocket. "I was on my way back to the office. It's nice to see you."

"And you too." She felt a little awkward and shy.

"Can I join you on your walk?"

"My walk? Oh sure. I had to get out of the store. Too much activity there. I needed to clear my head."

He stepped in line with her steps. It was as if they were on a Sunday stroll. Not that she'd ever done that, but she imagined this was what it would be like.

"What did Ebba say she would cook for us?"

"I'm not sure." She wondered if she could tell him about the spices that Ebba had used in their dishes last night.

"Should I call her?"

"No, I will. She and I need to talk."

"Talk? Did something happen?"

She stopped in the middle of the sidewalk, causing him to turn back to her. "What is going on here, Eamon? Is this what couples do? Are we a couple?"

He took her hand into his. "I'd like to think we are. I

know we've only had one real date, but I really, really like you. I had to tell the other officers we were dating."

"Sorry. I'm just very confused right now. My store gets broken into. I met you. Ebba, who I just met too, has the same picture I have of us as babies. Then she said she'd been in my store before, but she hasn't. And then I find a sketch of a man, and she says that is her father."

Eamon pulled her into his arms and hugged her. She felt the tears falling. When they had started, she didn't know.

"Opaline, it's okay. I'm here." He released her and led her to a bench in front of the hardware store. "If you need me to help you solve anything, let me know. I have a lot of connections in The Cities. I can call in favors."

"That is so nice. Thank you. My life is good as it could be. I mean, normal. Yes, I have money problems. Owning your own business is like that. But in forty-eight hours, it's been turned upside down."

"I'm going to call in to the office and tell them I'm taking the rest of the day off. I'll walk you back to the store, then I need to do a couple of things before coming back." He turned her head toward him. "That is, if you think I might need something for later."

"Yes," she said and kissed him. When their lips met, she felt as if time had stopped, and they were already in her bed making love.

He broke away first and stared at her. "I wish I had come back to you this morning."

"We'll have all night."

They stood, and he walked her back to the store. "Okay. I'll see you in about an hour."

She nodded and went inside. Her mind was still in a

frenzy, but the unanswered questions from earlier didn't mean as much to her now.

Paula came over to her. "Was that Eamon?"

"Yes. He has a few errands to do, then he'll be back."

"Interesting. Just to let you know, the front window is going to be installed this afternoon. I have to run over to Ebba's to pick up lunch for everyone. She made sandwiches again."

"She is wonderful. I'm never going to be able to repay her. I'll stay here. I never made the calls I wanted to earlier so I'll make them now."

Taking a few minutes, she walked through the store. Everyone greeted her as she passed them. Her heart swelled with joy at seeing the progress. Returning to the counter, she used the register to log on to the internet. The first email she sent was to Mr. Horton about her upcoming event, asking when the payment for the first one would be sent. She needed the money to pay for the new front window and the security system Eamon wanted her to purchase.

The next email was to her insurance company about filing a claim. Before she could make any calls to her vendors, Paula arrived with the food.

twenty-five

Upon awakening, Alyaaluladonati knew something had changed again. Breathing in and out deeply to clear his fogged mind, he felt the weak traces of energy in the room. He saw that the place where he hid his book was shimmering, which meant he had a message.

Quickly getting to his feet, he went to it. Pulling it from its hiding spot, he opened the memory book.

The council is divided. The prediction book is now saying new ancient ones will rule the council.

Rereading the cursive message, he let his human mask drop. His skin was now full of scales. Using his free hand, he touched his face. His long whiskers curled around his fingers. The horns that had grown when he had killed witches for the first time were warm to the touch.

He hadn't always looked this way. It was part of his curse. Every time he killed, a new and grotesque feature appeared. This, however, was the first time in a long time he had allowed his human mask to fully drop. Walking over to the table, he set the book down and picked up the pen.

That is not possible. I am the true leader. I will return.

He regretted writing the message after. He was about to write more to justify his response, but he heard voices downstairs. Closing the book and replacing it in its hiding spot, he crept toward the stairs, and his human mask covered him again.

From his position, Alyaaluladonati saw that the stupid owner had company. Using a little of his power, he used it to see through the walls and saw that the someone was none other than Opaline's other half, the police officer.

As he waited and listened, he felt the small exchange of power. It could only mean that the human who owned the house was one of his daughters' other halves.

But which one?

This was a new development—and an unexpected one. The three were now five.

The owner had called the police on him.

Stupid.

With a snap of his fingers, he could kill them both. But he couldn't; he needed them. Opaline's other half left, but he walked around the house. The owner stayed inside the house, and he heard him using a machine.

Once again, all was calm. The little surge of energy had been short-lived. Retracing his steps, he retrieved the book. This time, he sat for a few moments, thinking about what to write. The book had said new ancient ones would rule the council.

He thought of each member, and they each became a strand of thought. They wove themselves around each new one. Soon, the thread was thick. Each member of the ancient ones was now tightly intertwined with the others.

Touching the empty space on the front cover of the book, blue and white streams coiled around his hand. With his other hand, he placed two fingers on his temples. The blue and white streams found the thick thread in his mind and formed a cocoon around it.

He could hear their screams, feel their fear. Smiling, he made the blue and white streams pull tight, cutting off the threads.

All the members of the ancient ones left on his plane were now nonexistent. Alyaaluladonati consumed their power, giving him a super boost of energy. No one dared to challenge his right. By eliminating any possible challengers, he now stood stronger.

Opening the book, he wrote, *Feel my power. I am the one and only true leader.*

twenty-six

One by one, the customers who had turned into workers left, leaving only Paula and herself. Opaline walked through the aisles of bookshelves. She ran her hand over the books, loving the feel of them against her fingers.

The store looked fabulous.

The last touch, the front window, had been installed, and someone had painted around the border. It, too, was perfect. Looking out onto Main Street, she saw it wasn't busy. Not many people were out and about today, which was typical for a Friday.

"I have a couple of showings later this afternoon. If you don't need me, I'm going to head out," Paula said.

Opaline looked over at her. "Oh goodness, yes. You could have left at any time. I hate to think I've kept you from your clients."

"All's good. The window really makes the store bright and cheerful. It has wiped away all the ugliness of the mess."

Walking over to the front door, Opaline couldn't help but notice how new her store appeared. Paula was right. When customers came in, they would never know the store had been trashed a couple of days ago. "I'm thinking of having a grand reopening event once my shipments arrive."

"What a great idea. I can post it on my Facebook page for you. Just give me the date when you decide on one." Paula came over to the front door with her purse on her shoulder.

"We never talked—"

"I told you this morning we were to never speak of it."

"But I want you to know that I'm really interested in your brother."

"For real? Like I couldn't tell. You don't need my approval to date him." Paula shook her head, opened the door, and laughed. "Gotta go. See you later, Lady Godiva."

A brief flash of embarrassment came over her. Then, just like that, Opaline was alone in the store. There wasn't much that needed to be done. Maybe some dusting and vacuuming, but that could wait.

The sitting room beckoned her. Something in there had spooked Ebba. She'd said it was giving her bad vibes before she had rushed out of the store.

Walking over to it, the room looked like it always had. Mystical.

The initials etched into the glass caught her attention. Now that she knew they were there, she couldn't believe she had missed them all these years. They were as plain as day.

Sitting on the couch, she took a few of the stones out of the basket and laid them on the table. She placed her left hand on the stone in the necklace around her neck and began to sing the song her mother would sing to her.

"Hush, hush, my precious jewel. Everything will be all right. No more tears. The day will turn bright. The evil will disappear by candlelight. Hush, hush, my precious jewel."

A burst of light shone into the room, almost blinding her. Thinking it was the afternoon sunlight from the newly installed front window, Opaline sang the verse again. She closed her eyes. Before she could finish it, a feeling of calmness overcame her. A warmth encased her, and she breathed in deeply. Then an image of her mother reaching out to her came to her.

"Darling, it's time for you to remember. Be strong. Be vigilant."

Opaline opened her eyes. She searched the room for her mother. The voice had been so real, as if she was right next to her.

But it was empty.

The bright light was gone too. Three of the stones she had laid on the table were now stacked on top of each other. Confused, she took the top one off.

The second her fingers touched it, a wave of memories came over her. She saw herself as a little girl, in this room with two other girls around the table. They were laughing and playing with the stones, lining them up in different patterns.

The memory began to fade.

Curiosity got the better of her, and she took the second stone off the other one. Again, a long-forgotten memory came to her.

Her mother sat with her as they placed the stones in odd

patterns. "Only remember this time when you need to. You, my daughter, are a witch. The power you have is special. If that time is now, may the bindings I put on you be freed."

A coldness mixed with sadness settled over her. The vision of her mother vanished and was replaced with a swell of flashback recollections.

This room had been used by her mother and two other ladies. The ladies each had daughters. She now remembered all the mystical things that had happened in this room—from the strange lights to the singing.

Her mother had indeed been a witch.

Pensively, she thought about why this memory was only just now coming to her. The realization brought on several questions.

If her mother had been a witch, what kind had she been? Did powers come with being one?

A witch?

It couldn't be true. Witches were make believe.

She battled the questions and myths. Her mother couldn't have been a mean one, like in the horror stories, but one who did good for others. Her mother's words had said something about a binding spell.

I'm a witch too?

A binding spell? Why would her mother have done that?

But now little things began to have a purpose and made sense. Like the reason her mother had taught her about the string and tying knots in it. That explained why things would happen when she used the string.

And the forbidden use of certain words came back to her. "Blessed be." "Goodness within and goodness alive."

"Bright blessing and merry merry." They all had meanings and ramifications when used by a witch.

Her quiet life was being upheaved and turned inside out. Not able to fully comprehend what she was seeing or hearing, she stared at the last stone on the table.

Should she touch it?

Deep down, she'd always thought something was missing in her life. It was like when she'd start a puzzle and the last piece to make it complete had disappeared.

Could her interest in the mystical world be that missing piece?

Breathing deeply again and exhaling, she leaned over and touched the third stone. This time, a huge spark of electricity hit her fingers, throwing her backward on the couch. A green mist spewed from the stone. It filled the room, and she saw her mother holding hands with the other two ladies. They were each very pregnant. They spoke, but she couldn't hear them. Suddenly, a man appeared inside the circle. He laughed at them and snapped his fingers. Her mother and the other ladies fell to the ground, clutching their stomachs and screaming.

"Opaline? Are you in here?"

The green mist vanished, and so did the scene in front of her.

"Opaline? The door was open."

Eamon.

As if she'd been asleep, she jumped to her feet, knocking down the table with the stones on it. The three stones she had touched flew in three different directions and landed on the floor, while the others remained on the table.

"I'm in here. Over in the sitting room."

He appeared just inside the doorway and held the curtain in one hand. "Are you okay? I called your name a few times and locked the door. I was about to head upstairs to find you."

"The strangest thing just happened. Come over here." She stood and debated whether to share her experience with him. But she trusted him and knew he wouldn't judge her, even though she saw his concern in his narrowed eyes and clenched jaw. "I don't know how to say this, but I had a vision. It was of my mother. She told me I was a witch. Can you believe that? I'm a witch. And so was she."

"Calm down. You should sit. You're as white as a ghost."

He took her hands and led her back to the couch. Eamon sat next to her holding her hands. "I'm not a believer of the unnatural stuff. But I've seen things that can't be explained. Tell me what happened."

"Everyone had left the store. Then I remembered Ebba had gotten freaked out by something in here. So I sat down, like we are now. I was playing with the stones in the basket—"

"Take a breath. You're talking very fast."

She did what he said. He was right. She was overly excited, and all her emotions were on high alert. Even now, as he held her hands, she felt his heart beating faster too. She smelled his male testosterone, which was making her physically aware of him.

Freeing her hands from his, she folded them on her lap. "I placed the stones on the table, and then something happened. I can't explain it, but then three of the stones were on top of each other, stacked. I reached out and touched the top one, and then I saw my mother. She told me I was a witch."

"I've heard of people having visions of loved ones they had lost before."

"This was different. I can see—no, understand—things now. It's like I had a veil over me, and it's now gone." She took his hand into hers. "Like when I touch you, I get this feeling—no, a sense—that we are meant to be together. I can see us—"

"Opaline, what kind of stones are they? Could they have a coating on them that is a drug of some sort?"

Releasing his hand, she stood. "Are you making fun of me? Are you suggesting that I'm selling illegal drugs? I'm telling you something happened to me in this very room because I touched the stones."

"I'm not making fun of you. Let's try to recreate it. The detective inside me wants to know the truth, wherever it may lead."

But as she stared at him, all she could think about was making love to him. Her pheromones were in overdrive. She sure hoped he'd come prepared this time.

Joining him once again on the couch, she kissed him. She felt his hesitance, but when she placed her hand on his thigh and moved it upward to his groin, he pulled her close. Her hunger for him was more of an urgency.

She ended the kiss and nudged him backward so that they were lying on the couch. Moving so she was in between his legs, half sitting, she unbuttoned his shirt, exposing his broad and muscular chest. She admired his tempting male physique. Even with the shirt opened, his shoulders and arms were strained against the thin fabric.

"Opaline?"

"I've waited all day for this."

Ignoring his questioning tone, she leaned over and kissed one of his nipples. She slid her hands over his six-pack and heard him moan. This aroused her own passion. She felt his hands skimming over her thighs and then moving under her dress. His fingers slipped under her panties. Any resolve she had left weakened beneath his exploring touch.

"Should we go upstairs?"

The telltale sign of his own desire was pressed against her.

"No more delays. I want you now," she said.

Her words had the sought-after effect. He pulled her dress upward. She raised her arms, allowing him to slip it off of her. Moving so that his legs were free, Eamon stood and unfastened his belt. Unzipping his pants, they fell to his feet, but he couldn't get them over his shoes, causing him to sit down.

Opaline laughed.

"Not my best act of stripping. Like I said, I'm out of practice." He bent over, untied his shoes, and took them off, allowing the pants to be freed. Taking them in his hands, he was about to throw them but instead dug into the front pocket, withdrawing a packet of condoms.

"Now we're talking." Opaline unhooked her bra and slipped off her panties.

Eamon stood again and took off his shirt along with his underwear.

They faced each other.

"You're beautiful."

"You're handsome." A brief sense of shyness came over

her, but when he reached out and brushed wisps of her hair away from her face, it disappeared.

His hand drifted downward, caressing her, and then he cupped her breast. She stared at him while his other hand magically moved over her other breast, bringing the nipple taut.

She exhaled sharply.

Her other breast ached for his attention. And as if he knew, he cupped it with possessiveness and tantalized that nipple. Then he leaned down and took one nipple into his mouth, sucking it.

She had to place her hands on his shoulders for support as waves of pleasure filled her. He released the now-sensitive nipple and kissed a fiery path downward over her stomach. Knowing where he was heading, she shifted to allow him to find what he sought.

But he didn't go where she thought he was going. He stopped his kisses and stood. "Sit on the couch."

She sat as he pushed the table away. He squatted down in front of her. This time, she knew what he wanted her to do. Opening her legs wide, he positioned himself in between them and placed her legs on his shoulders. He kissed her left inner thigh and then moved to the right one.

An involuntary tremor set off when his lips began a sensuous path inward. She reached a spiral of desire when his mouth and tongue reached its destination.

"Oh, Eamon."

Tiny explosives of ecstasy flooded through her veins when his tongue pressed and licked her nub until she cried out. A million stars exploded in her.

Before she could recover, he lifted her legs off his

shoulders and tugged her upright. They stood again, facing each other. He kissed her and lifted her upward. She wrapped her arms around his neck and her legs around his waist as he pushed his hardness into her.

"You're full of surprises," she whispered into his ear and then kissed his neck.

Eamon took ahold of her hips and lifted her up and down over his hardness, filling her as he tried to reach her special spot. He filled her completely.

"No, my sweet Opaline, you're the one who is full of surprises."

She never dreamed a man would make her feel this many bursts of desire. He pushed and pushed until she felt him touch her core. Her body trembled from the vibrating, burning sweetness. She abandoned all strings of her resolve, allowing the whirl of sensations to come over her.

"Goodness alive!" she screamed as the orgasm's hot tide raged through her. From some other plane, she felt him take his own release. Opaline opened her eyes and found Eamon staring at her, but they were fully dressed and not in the sitting room in the bookstore. "Eamon?"

"What's going on, Opaline?"

They stood side by side but not in the throngs of passion. She was wearing some sort of costume. The dress was white and gold and hung off one shoulder. Eamon was wearing some sort of Roman military outfit, which was also in white and gold.

"I'm not sure. Maybe my witch powers have taken us someplace. Hold my hand. Don't let go of it, no matter what you see." She remembered her mother telling her that sometimes.

He gripped her hand tightly.

Suddenly, the area around them began to fill with people. They were wearing similar outfits but in different colors. Not sure what to do, she pressed her mind for answers. She saw a woman come to them and gasped. It was her mother.

"My darling, you can't be here. It is not time. May the gods protect you. Go now."

A bright light exploded around them. She gripped Eamon's hand when she felt his slipping away from hers. Then, just like that, she was naked, wrapped in his embrace in the bookstore.

"Oh my god, Eamon, did you see that?"

He lifted her off of him and set her on the couch. Removing the condom, he placed it on his underwear and joined her. She noted his eyes were wide.

"That was a first for me. I can't explain what just happened. Did you see all those people? They were bowing down to us."

"You did see it too! Did you hear my mother? She sent us back here."

"I did hear a woman." He ran his hands over his chin and mouth. "Opaline, did you put a spell on me?"

"No. I swear I didn't."

The whole situation seemed like a dream. Had she fallen asleep on the couch in the sitting room? Why would she have had sex with Eamon in her store during the day?

But it wasn't a dream. They were naked as the day they were born, talking about spells.

twenty-seven

Eamon was totally out of his element with being naked in a bookstore. He stood and reached for his pants. "Not to ruin our first time together, but I think we should get dressed. With all the lights on, someone outside might see us. I can't be arrested for indecent exposure."

What he didn't say was that he had an officer outside keeping taps on the bookstore. And he didn't want that person to see what he was doing in his personal time.

"Right. I've never done this before...here in... Let's get dressed and go upstairs." Opaline slipped on her dress and picked up her panties and bra. "I better lock the door."

"No need. I did when I came in." He noticed Opaline looked a little flushed. But who wouldn't be, by having sex in the middle of her place of business?

"Thank you. What time is it?"

"Four thirty," Eamon said as he looked at his phone. "We should think about dinner. Didn't you say Ebba was going to have something to-go for us?"

"I'm sorry. I wanted our-our first time together to be special."

"And being taken to a different world wasn't? I think our first time was very special. And by the way, I have more condoms." He pulled some out and held them up, hoping his own embarrassment wasn't coming across to her. Having sex in the middle of the day in her store wasn't what he planned for their first time. Still, trying to understand what had happened to them wasn't working. None of his weird or unexplained cases had prepared him for what he'd seen or experienced.

"Oh, you do, do you? I think we should see what Ebba has made for us. You might need the food for strength. I plan on making use of however many you have with you."

Her comment made him take a second look at Opaline. He couldn't help but admire the woman who had made him feel things he hadn't thought possible. She was like no one he'd ever known. Bright, funny, and an apparent insatiable sexual appetite.

Following her to the back of the store and to the stairs, he couldn't help but notice the sway of her hips. He had to clear his throat to rein in his thoughts of wanting her again so soon.

She flipped the light switches, and the area became dark. Pushing the curtain aside, they went up the stairs. When they reached the upper door, her cat, Athena, was waiting and meowing, just like the night before.

"I brought him home again. I'll fix your dinner," Opaline called out as she opened the door. The cat rushed forward to them, weaving in and out of their legs. She picked her up and hugged her. "Come on in, Eamon. I have to feed Athena first before I text Ebba."

"Do you want me to call the restaurant?"

"She might not come to the phone. Fridays are very busy for her, 'she said.' It'll only take a minute to feed Athena. Take a seat in the living room."

"I think I'll use the bathroom, if you don't mind. And I need to throw these away."

She looked over at him. He was holding out his underwear that had the used condom in it.

"Are you a commando kind of guy?"

"I am today." He laughed and tugged on the crotch of his pants. As much as a pain in the ass underwear were, they did have a purpose of holding in certain things.

"Under the sink in here or the bathroom, which is to your left and down the hall."

Choosing the bathroom would allow him some privacy and time to clean himself up. Inside, he took a few minutes to wash himself after disposing of the condom into the toilet and tossing his underwear in the trash can.

Why had he let his primitive behavior take over? He'd been like a stag during rutting. Never with another woman had he acted like he did just a few minutes ago with Opaline. Feeling a little guilty, he told himself he was going to take his time and show her just how much he loved her next time.

Loved her? Where had that come from?

How could he love her already? They'd only met three days ago. But here he was, professing his love for her in the mirror.

Was there really something to this whole witch and spells angle? Had she put a spell on him?

Witchcraft was a thing. He'd learned about it in the academy but hadn't been privy to any cases that involved someone claiming to be one. A cynical inner voice weighed the questions; however, no answers came.

After placing his used washcloth on the towel rack, he walked out of the bathroom and met Opaline in the hallway.

"Done so soon?"

"As a matter of fact, yes. I am really hungry."

She laughed, and the sound lightened the mood. He knew she had caught on to his play on words. He saw she had put on her bra but couldn't tell if she wore any panties. He cleared his throat again to reign in his sexual feelings, then he took her hand.

"Do we have time before the food arrives?"

"My, my, you are hungry. Actually, we have to go pick it up. She wouldn't tell me what it was."

He leaned in and kissed her, drawing her in against his body. "I guess I'll—we'll—have to wait. I'll go now and get it, or it will be cold if I have my way."

She kissed him and ran her hand over his butt and pinched it.

"Ouch. What was that for?"

"Checking to see if you were still going commando."

"I am." He followed her back to the kitchen and saw Athena was almost finished with her dinner. The cat glanced up at him. He thought he'd seen her wink. It couldn't have been possible, but he was sure the cat had. "I'll head out to get our dinner. Should I pick up a bottle of wine?"

"I have a couple, a Chateau blend and a Caymus. It's going to depend on whether she made fish or meat. You should use the back stairs since the store is closed."

"Both of those wines sound fantastic. See you in a few."

She rushed over to him and wrapped her arms around his neck and kissed him again.

Her unexpected action had him pulling her closer. Had she changed her mind?

Their lips teased each other's mouths. Their tongues touched in a sensual way, and then the kiss ended.

"What was that for? Not that I'm complaining."

"Just wanted you to hurry back," she said.

"You don't have to worry about that. I'm under your spell."

"I didn't put one on you. Plus, I don't think love spells work."

They stared at each other. The four-letter word hung in the air.

She'd said *love*. But it hadn't been used in the same context in which he was thinking about it in the bathroom. It was used as an overall word.

"I better get going."

"Right. I'll set the table."

He nodded, ignoring the word she had used, and walked out using the back stairs. Once he cleared the building, he walked over to the unmarked police car that was positioned across the street.

"Hey, Officer Dayan."

"Thanks for doing this, Officer Warren. I wanted to let you know that I'll be spending some time with Ms. Lunn tonight. If you could walk the perimeter about every hour or so, that would be great. Remember, the backyard is where we found the footprints. I'm going to pick up some dinner for her and me, do you want me to get something for you too?"

"No, sir. I have all I need here." He pointed to a cooler sitting on the front seat.

"Okay, then. I'll have my phone on. Text or call if you spot anything abnormal."

"Will do. Have a good night."

Eamon nodded and made his way back across the street to Mignon's Place. When he got inside, he saw the man who had called about an intruder earlier today. "Hello, Mr. Waters, any more trouble since this afternoon?"

"No. Everything has been quiet. Just waiting for my date."

"I'm picking up some to-go entrees."

The hostess handed him a huge bag. "The chef said to enjoy what she made for you."

"Thank you. I'm sure we will. By the way, can you let her know that Mr. Waters and his date are friends of mine?"

"By all means, of course," the hostess said.

"Thanks again, Officer Dayan. Oh, my date just walked in."

Eamon moved to the side and saw a woman with black hair come into the restaurant. She didn't look familiar, but there was something in her mannerisms that triggered a connection. Owin pushed past him to greet the woman, dismissing him.

Smiling, he ignored the brush-off and left. He had his own mind on a woman, and she was waiting for his return. With hurried steps, he walked down the street.

twenty-eight

Opaline watched the sexiest man she ever knew leave. She plopped down on the couch and closed her eyes. Her mind wouldn't quiet down. Thought after thought roamed around in it. Before she could absorb one thought, another would seep in.

What happened when she and Eamon climaxed? They'd actually gone to another realm of some sort. She knew she hadn't imagined it because Eamon had mentioned being taken to another place.

Her mother had been there and sent them back. She'd said it wasn't time. Time for what?

Athena joined her on the couch, and she opened her eyes and began to stroke her along the neck and back. More thoughts of Eamon ran rampant in her head.

He was perfect for her and so thoughtful. His ability to make her feel confident and sure of herself was a huge plus. Then there was this feeling of being in love that wouldn't go away.

"I think I'm in love with him, Athena."

Her phone vibrated. Looking at it, she saw it was from Ebba. She had texted her while Eamon had used the bathroom.

EBBA:

> I made baked chicken. With basil. A touch of fennel seed with some orange peels. And for dessert, fresh raspberry tarts that I adorned with their leaves. I added my blessing and love.

What could all those herbs mean? Was Ebba adding some more things to their dinner to make these feelings manifest or come to light? After reading the text, Opaline tapped Call. The line rang and rang, and then Ebba answered.

"I thought that might get your attention. What's up?"

"We have to talk. I mean, talk about our mothers and the room in my store. Something happened. I can't...I don't understand it. I saw my mother."

"Slow down. I'm stepping out of the kitchen." There was a long pause, and Ebba came back. "What happened?"

"No, I can't get into it now. Can you come over tomorrow?"

"Sure. Do you want me to make breakfast? Will it be for two or three?"

Opaline laughed. "It could be for three. I'll talk to Eamon about it and text you what time to come over."

"Sounds good. I've been thinking about the room too. I might have something that could help us. Sorry, Opaline. I have to get back to the kitchen."

"Right. Thanks. Bye."

"Bye."

She held the phone in her hand as Athena decided to sit on her lap. "What's up, girl? Do you feel the air is different since Eamon has been here? Have I put a spell on him?"

Meow. Meow.

"I couldn't have. I don't know how to do spells. Those memories I do know to be true. Mother never taught me any. But could she have left me instructions? Is that what you're trying to tell me?"

Meow.

"Okay. Let's go see what we can find in that box." Lifting Athena into her arms, she left the couch and went into her bedroom. "Oh no, crap."

Papers and other items from her mother's box were scattered across the bed.

"Athena, is this what you were trying to tell me?"

The cat wiggled out of her arms and jumped down onto the bed. *Meow. Meow. Meow.*

"What is it? I have to clean up everything before Eamon gets back." Hurriedly, Opalina gathered all the papers into a pile. But Athena refused to budge off of a book. "Come on, girl. Eamon is going to be here soon."

She had to pick up Athena and move her. The book looked older than Earth itself. Where had it come from? She didn't remember placing it on the bed earlier this morning.

Picking it up, she held it. Running her hand over the cover, she noted it was leather and had an unusual indentation in the middle. With two fingers, she traced the odd figure.

Athena began to purr loudly and nudged her hand. She felt an odd warming sensation on her chest. Setting the book down, she touched the stone in her necklace. It was the source of the heat. She looked downward and saw the bluish stone was glowing. With one hand cupping the stone and her other hand on the indentation in the book, she forced herself to stay calm.

The blues in the pendant began to swirl, forming a mist. It was pulling her into it, and she saw the place she'd seen with Eamon. She was in a hall. The floor was made of bricks. The walls were smooth with torches attached to them. Trying to see more, she concentrated.

Then she saw Ebba and another woman walking toward her, dressed in long gowns. They looked over their shoulders and began to run with their hands outstretched to her.

"Opaline. What is wrong?"

She closed her eyes and released the stone in her necklace to find Eamon next to her.

"Opaline, say something."

"Eamon, I'm fine."

"No, you're not. I've been standing next to you for about five minutes. Your pendant was glowing."

"It was?" She sat on the edge of the bed, refusing to look at the book lying next to her.

"What is going on? If this is some supernatural stuff, it's got me a little weirded out," Eamon said and sat on the bed next to her.

She looked over at him. At that moment, she knew that she did love him. Any other man would've walked out by now or called her crazy.

"I'm not sure what is happening to me, to us. But I do know that I love you. I know we've just met, but you and I are meant to be together. I know it."

"I'm surprised. I don't—"

"I'd understand if you left."

"What? No. I'm not leaving you. I feel the same way. I believe we are soulmates. I love you too."

She couldn't believe what he was saying. He loved her too!

"Let's forget about dinner. Let's have dessert now."

He stood, and with a sweep of his arm, he cleared off everything from the top of the bed. The book fell to the floor with a thud. She pushed herself backward on the bed, slid her dress off of her body, and unhooked her bra. Eamon joined her, naked too, on the bed.

"I promised myself to make love to you slowly, but I'm not sure I can live up to that promise."

"I think we'll have a lifetime of making love. All I want is you now."

She opened her legs, and he moved into the space she had created. He kissed her lips at the same time he slid into her.

Arching her hips, she took him in and battled his tongue with hers. The age-old rocking took over, and soon she felt the rising of her passion. There had been no sparks in her, only fire, and it was consuming every part of her body.

In and out, Eamon pushed. She met each thrust.

Releasing his lips, she screamed as the first orgasm overcame her in waves. Before the last wave ended, another orgasm formed. Her love for him consumed her desire.

Neither knew the moment their passion ended and began to form again. Their bodies and souls merged leaving hot tides of ecstasy to fulfill in electric swirls.

Eamon dislodged himself from Opaline. Trying not to make any noise, he took his phone out of his pants pocket and carried it out of the bedroom. After making a stop in the bathroom, he went to the kitchen. The bag of food from Ebba's restaurant sat on the counter, untouched.

He grinned, knowing he didn't need the food for strength.

First, he checked his phone for messages or phone calls. There were four text messages and two missed calls. The messages were all from Paula, which he ignored. One call was from the Minneapolis Police Station. Tapping the message, he read it. They had the results from the piece of cloth he'd found next to the fence behind Opaline's store. The other call was from Officer Warren, letting him know the same thing.

Brushing his hand through his hair, he leaned against the counter. He'd have to leave early again. Opaline wasn't going to be happy. After he'd found her in some sort of trance in her bedroom and their mad rush of sex, they'd never gotten around to eating the food.

twenty-nine

Opaline kissed Eamon goodbye as he walked out. Then she texted Ebba.

OPALINE

Sorry I didn't text last night. It's okay to come over. Breakfast for two only.

EBBA

Two. Am I not invited?

She smiled.

OPALINE

Eamon had to leave.

EBBA

He'll have to keep a set of clothes at your house. Be there in twenty minutes.

OPALINE

You can tell him the next time you see
him. Lol.

Again, the fact she'd gained a best friend in a matter of
a few days was crazy. She'd gone so long without any true
friendships because the store and her customers had been
her entire world. Hurriedly, she washed up, brushed her
teeth, and put on a little makeup. Tossing her robe on the
bed, she put on shorts and a T-shirt. Athena chose that
moment to show herself and begin meowing.

"Did I miss your breakfast time?" As she bent down to
pet her, she saw the old book on the floor, partly under the
bed. Taking it, she walked out to the living room and set it
on the table. Wanting to touch the indentation again,
however, she refrained from doing it, wanting Ebba to see
what happened when she did.

Checking her phone for emails, she saw one from Mr.
Horton and opened it. He thanked her for hosting the
event and indicated he'd be sending out her check tomorrow. He also reminded her to have another event as soon
as possible per their agreement and would get in touch
with her when he could meet her.

A knock on the door made her jump. Twenty minutes
had gone by?

Getting off the couch, she went to the door and felt her
cheeks become warm. Yesterday, she'd opened the door
naked, hoping it had been Eamon on the other side. This
time, when she opened the door, Ebba stood with her
arms full of bags of food.

"I didn't order groceries."

"Behave. I brought things to cook with since I knew

you wouldn't have what I needed. Good morning to you too."

"Come on in. My kitchen is now yours," she said and waved her arms.

Ebba ignored her flamboyant actions and walked past her. "Spill your guts. I see my dinners went uneaten. Didn't it taste good?"

"I'm so sorry about that. We did eat the dessert first and last." Her play on words describing what she and Eamon had done made Ebba stop taking things out of the bags and stare at her. "What?"

"You're getting spoiled, girl. Two desserts. I like this guy. I guess you didn't need any of my special ingredients."

They laughed, and Athena jumped up on the counter. Ebba pet her. "We have to find you a mate too."

"Oh no. One cat is enough for me. Unless you're going to get one."

"I'm never home to have any pets. I kill goldfish in like three days. I can't take care of them either."

"What are you making? I'm hungry." She picked up Athena and set her on the floor.

"Oh, you are? I would be too after all the exercise you've had. I thought we'd have French toast with blue-berry sauce. It won't take me long to fix it. What did you want to talk about? I'm sure it isn't about Eamon." Ebba took out a pan and bowl from the cupboards.

"Things have been happening. Strange things I don't understand. Like all of a sudden, this book, this very old book, appears in my mother's stuff. I've never ever seen it before in my life. It just appeared. Then things become even unfathomable. I can't believe I'm about to share this, but I have to tell you what happened when Eamon and I had sex."

"Stop. I don't need to know the details of you doing that. We are friends, but that is some TMI I don't need to know."

"But something life altering happened. And it pertains to when we were...when he and I... you know."

"Know what?"

Closing her eyes, Opaline inhaled, exhaled, and then counted to three before she spoke. "When Eamon and I climaxed, something happened."

"That isn't unusual. My goodness, girl. You do know about the birds and the bees and flowers, right?"

"I'm trying to be serious." She opened her eyes, took ahold of her necklace, and rubbed the stone. "At that moment, when we came, something... Suddenly, we were in another place. He saw and felt it too. We were in a huge hall. There were a lot of people, and my mother came up to me. She told me it was my time. And just like that, we were back in the sitting room."

"The sitting room, in the bookstore? You had sex down there?"

"Yes. I can't believe we did. It just all happened so fast. And there's more. After everyone had left the store, I went over to the table to look at your initials in the glass. I was playing with the stones in the baskets, and then out of nowhere, my mother appeared. She told me now was the time for me to remember. And I did. I saw you and me as little girls, playing with the stones. My mother was a witch, and I think I am too. Not that I know any spells or what it means, but I know I am." Opaline planted her hands on the counter and waited for Ebba to say something. After what seemed like an eternity, she finally stopped stirring what she was mixing in the bowl.

"Let me get this straight. Your mother appears to you. She tells you to remember, and you have this rush of memories. And because of these so-called memories, you think you're a witch?"

"Yes."

Ebba set the spoon down, moved closer to her, and then took her hands into hers. "I knew that room meant something to me. I think I'm a witch too. I've been having these weird dreams of my mother. She comes to me and tells me how all these herbs and other ingredients make things happen. I have a notepad on my nightstand, so I can write them down when I wake up."

Running her hands through her hair and pushing it behind her ears, Opaline shook her head. "That's not all. I saw my mother holding hands with two other ladies. All three of them were pregnant. I couldn't hear what they were saying. Then a man appeared in the middle of them, and the three women fell to the ground, holding their abdomens. I didn't get to see anymore. The vision vanished when Eamon called my name."

"Did your mom have any sisters? Mine didn't. But I think witches call other women in their group, or wiccan, sisters. I brought over the picture of my mom holding me. Let's compare them."

Opaline went back into the bedroom and picked up her mother's box. Athena, who'd been sleeping on the bed stirred and followed her out.

"Here are my mother's things. The old book is there on the table. See the indent on the front?"

"I see it. Should I touch it like you did?"

Joining Ebba on the couch, she took the book and placed it on her lap. "Get your phone ready to take a video. I was holding onto my mother's pendant."

"I'm wearing a necklace that was my mom's too." Ebba reached into the top of her shirt and withdrew an odd-shaped stone. "This was hers."

"It's beautiful. It's almost like mine."

They held out their stones. Ebba's was clear white, and hers was bluish. They were both encased in thin silver bands that cradled the stones.

"The same but different. Yours leans to the right, and mine leans to the left. Very strange. Anyways, I was holding my necklace while I traced the imprint on the book with my finger."

Ebba looked at her. "Okay, let's do this."

Opaline turned the book so Ebba had a better angle and pressed Record on her phone. Doing what she had said she'd done, Ebba took ahold of her pendant with her left hand and traced the indentation on the cover. Watching through her phone, nothing happened. Ebba just sat there tracing the odd shape with her fingers.

"Ebba, do you see anything? Or feel any different?"

"No. The leather seems dry."

Opaline set the book back on the table and ended the recording on her phone. Why hadn't it worked for Ebba, who thought she might be a witch? "Very odd. Let's look at the pictures again. Remember I told you my mother said something about binding me? Maybe yours did the same to you."

"Right, binding. I watched this series, which was based on some books about a girl's parents doing that to her to protect her," Ebba said and dug into her bag. "I'm planning on doing some research on demons and gods. I don't think the people I saw were human. Or if they were, they weren't from this universe. You know, like in the Marvel movies when they travel to multi-universes."

"You watch that stuff?"

"I do. I find it fascinating."

Ebba held out two pictures. One of a man and the other of her mother, holding her as a baby.

"Look at this. My picture with the three ladies sitting on a bench looks like the same bench in your picture of you as a baby." Opaline held out her picture.

Together, they compared the scenery and determined it was the same season since the trees in the background had leaves on them. They set the pictures aside and decided to open the book.

"Since it seems to have a connection with me, I'll open it and turn the pages. Now it's your turn to have the phone ready to capture anything that might happen."

"I feel like a TikTok person." Ebba laughed and tapped the video button on her phone.

Opaline opened the book. The first page had a single word on it, *one*. She turned the page, and it had the letter *O* on it and nothing else. Looking at Ebba, she shrugged her shoulders. "Very odd."

Turning that page, the next one revealed a picture of the book they were looking at with the title, Ancient Ones. But the book pictured had a heart in the center. Keeping her finger on the page, Opaline looked at the cover.

"I see it now. The indentation is in the shape of a heart incased in a circle," Ebba stated.

"I've never seen this in my mother's things. I'm really

confused because I don't recall seeing this book before last night."

"Maybe we're like the Charmed Ones in the television series from years ago. Could this be your book of spells? If your mother appeared and your bindings have been freed, maybe that is why, and how, the book came to you."

Opaline sat back on the couch, and Athena jumped onto her lap. "Girl, now is not the time. I'm busy."

Athena meowed and walked onto the top of the book and proceeded to scratch the cover with her claws.

"Stop! Don't do that!" Opaline yelled. Athena arched her spine and hissed at her. She picked her up and held her, petting her to calm her. "What has gotten into you, girl? Behave."

"That was freaky. Something could have spooked her."

"Perhaps the smell of the leather triggered her. I'll have to cover it when I put it away. I'm getting myself a bottle of water. Do you want one too?"

"I could use one, thanks. I've been thinking. The only other thing in your life that has changed is that you met Eamon. Could he have something to do with all this too?"

"No way." She set Athena down in the kitchen and gave her some treats.

Ebba did have a good point. Could Eamon have something to do with what has been happening to her? He did seem to be around whenever something inexplicable occurred.

"If we're taking leaps here, what about the break-in? What could the person have been looking for? This book?" She held up the old book.

"I think you're on to something. Since your bookstore was torn apart, I'll bet the person was looking for it."

Opaline's phone buzzed. She looked at it and saw Eamon had texted. She read it aloud. "I have to stay longer than I thought. Call you on my way home."

"Oh, how sweet."

"Stop it, Ebba. He's being thoughtful."

"It just gives us more time to solve this puzzle. Who could the House of Ancients be? I mean, I've never heard of them in Greek anthology."

"I know this... I remember this." Opaline picked up the book and began to flip through the pages. "The House of Ancients is the bloodline of the gods who rule the other universe. There are three factions—the Ancients, the Artefacts, and the Antigods—which make up the Council of Gods."

"Who are you? How do you know this?"

"I told you. I remember everything now. My mother used to tell me stories about another land. There were princesses and princes. Sometimes the world she talked about seemed real. This is very exciting."

"Maybe for you. It still doesn't answer why your mother had a sketch of my father in her things."

"Right. We got off track." Opaline closed the book and set it back down. "When is your birthday? Mine is November eleventh."

"No way. That is mine too. How strange it is that we both have the same birthday, and we live in the same town. Let's google to see how many babies were born that year and date."

"Right. If you and I are connected, could there be others? Do you have your birth certificate? I've never been able to find mine."

"I don't have one either. We can google that too. Let's get copies of them."

Together, they worked on the computer and made notes on what they found. The more and more they dug, it only led to more questions and down rabbit holes.

PAULA

Where are you?

Eamon ignored the text message from his sister. He didn't have time to deal with her.

"Sir, I have the results for the Onamia Police Department. Please sign here for them."

He took the pen from the officer and signed his name. The Minneapolis Police Department did everything by the book. No leeway for anything since all the riots a few years ago. Taking the packet, he walked out of the building and back to his car.

Back inside his car, he called Paula.

"Hello. It's about time."

"I'm on police business. I don't need to tell you every time I leave."

"I know. I was about to go see Opaline and didn't want a repeat of the other day."

He shook his head and sighed. She wasn't going to ever let him forget that she knew he had slept over at Opaline's. "I had to drive down to The Cities for some evidence. I'll be back in a few hours. While I'm down here, is there anything you need?"

"Thanks for asking, but I'm fine. I have a busy afternoon. I leased the empty location just down from Opaline's store. The lady is coming over to the office to sign the papers."

He started the car, and the call connected to the Bluetooth. "That's great. I'll see you later for dinner."

"Dinner? Are you cooking?"

"No. You are. Bye." Without waiting for his sister to reply, he ended the call and smiled. He knew she wouldn't cook anything. He'd been teasing her.

As he drove back to Onamia, the traffic was light until he hit the St. Cloud exits. Taking the back roads to avoid most of it gave him time to go over what had happened to him and Opaline in the middle of having sex.

Being taken to another place, or universe, was something he was still trying to wrap his fingers around. And then there had been Mr. Waters' intruder and what had happened there.

He felt like he was in some twilight zone movie. Unnatural and strange phenomena weren't his thing or expertise. He didn't even know anyone he could contact.

His phone rang, and he saw it was the office. He tapped Answer on the car's console. "Hello, this is Officer Dayan."

"I hate to bother you on a Sunday, but Mr. Waters called in again and asked for you."

"I think I have his number. Can you text it to me? I'm driving."

"Yes. He wouldn't say why he wanted to talk to you."

"That's okay. I'll call him when I get the number."

They hung up, and a minute later, his phone dinged. Tapping the console, the number appeared. Then he tapped the number, and the phone rang.

"Hello?"

"Hi, this is Officer Dayan. What can I do for you?"

"Thanks for calling me back. I know we chatted a little bit last night at the restaurant, but I saw something this morning. There was a bright, bluish light coming from the attic, and a power surge fried my circuit breakers."

"But you didn't see anyone?"

"No. I went up to the attic, but it showed no signs of anyone being there. It's not much, but you said to let you know if anything unusual happened."

Eamon turned on his blinker and merged into the next lane. "I appreciate it. If you can take some pictures of the circuit breakers, you can email them to me."

"I can do that. I was wondering, since I work during the week, if you can have someone drive by my place a few times."

Stopping for a red light, Eamon tapped the steering wheel. The department didn't have people he could send, but it was a good idea. "I'll do it personally since I'm familiar with the case. Thanks for letting me know."

"No, thank you for taking this seriously. Most people would brush it off. You have a good day."

Eamon told him to have one too and ended the call just as he was turning onto Main Street. Checking the time, he decided to head home to shower before going back to Opaline's.

thirty

Feeling an energy surge, Alyaaluladonati awoke. Not sure what had happened, he quickly exited his makeshift bed. Not sensing anyone, he checked the protection wards he had put up to hide the room from human eyes.

Then he saw it. The space on the wall to hold his book was empty. The book was gone.

But how could it have been freed?

With each step he took, he felt a weakness in his bones. Someone had stolen his source of power.

Damn it!

All of his carefully organized plans had been ruined. He would need to confront Opaline and take some of her power until he could find his book.

Breathing hard, he tried to control his anger. This had never happened before. To lose the book was dangerous.

But who had taken it?

Then it dawned on him. If Opaline had committed

herself to her soulmate, she could've had enough power to call the book to her.

With hurried steps, he left the rundown farmhouse and headed into town. The bitch was going to give him his book back. She couldn't have it.

As he surveyed the street and the bookstore building, he saw Eamon's black car arrive. Using some of his energy to shield himself from everyone, he followed Eamon to the front door of the store.

Eamon knocked, and Opaline opened the door. When she leaned in and kissed Eamon, her aura was powerful. He saw the energy the two of them created with just the touch of their lips. To have that amount of energy would last centuries here in this world.

Mercy!

Alyaaluladonati couldn't help but smile with glee. If these two had that vitality potency, what would the other four create?

Stepping around the pair locked in a kiss, he murmured, "Come to me. You are mine, not hers."

Suddenly, a screech echoed inside the store. Opaline and Eamon broke apart.

"Ebba, what's wrong?" Opaline ran to a small room. Eamon followed.

"The book began to shimmer," Ebba stated.

"Did you see anything? Feel anything?" Opaline asked.

"No, it just frightened me. Here, you take it. This whole witch thing is getting scary."

Opaline took the book from Ebba. Eamon came and stood next to Opaline and touched her hand.

Alyaaluladonati couldn't believe what was going on. Opaline had indeed gotten her powers. He was about to call for the book again, but he hesitated when Opaline opened it. Then the three of them were taken to his universe.

Unable to stop it, he was forced into his world along with them. Thinking he'd made it without the stones and his other two daughters, he was about to celebrate.

"Thank you for bringing me home," he said.

Opaline and Eamon turned to stare at him.

"Who are you?" Eamon demanded, still clutching Opaline's hand.

"Someone you should be very afraid of." He felt his world's power seep into his every pore. He lifted his hand to kill them, but he was momentarily frozen in place.

"You are not allowed here. My daughter will not die by your hand."

"Mother, what is going on? Who is this man?" Opaline asked.

"That is your father. He has been banished from this world, the one you are in right now, the world that saved me. But he has been trying to return for years. He has been trying to siphon off power from witches to find his way back here and to protect himself in our—your—world. His end game is to return to this world along with the power of the ONE. Don't let him succeed."

"But I'm not a witch or warlock, why am I here?" Eamon asked.

"Because he figured out why none of the other witches' powers were strong enough to send him back. The witches need their soulmates. You are my daughter's soulmate."

Alyaaluladonati laughed, still frozen in place. The three finally looked at him.

"Yes, I did. Nevaeh, you were always the missing piece.

By naming your daughter the leader, I watched her after I killed you. I knew she would find the others and bring them to me. It is always this way. But their soulmates only make them stronger, which I need."

Thunder and lightning echoed in the halls. Alyaalu-ladonati looked upward and saw the other gods coming for them. His universe's energy poured into his being. Whatever little spell Nevaeh had used wasn't strong enough to hold him. In one swift move, he grabbed at the book. He struggled with his daughter to free it from her grip.

"No, you can't have it!" Opaline yelled.

"Give it to me. It's mine. I am the Ancient One." His command did not affect her. Glancing upward, he knew he didn't have much time and yanked harder.

"Leave us alone," Eamon said.

"You're simply a human you have no powers here. You are like dirt."

Eamon shoved him while still holding onto Opaline. The three of them struggled. Then he saw his stone around Opaline's neck.

She saw his eyes shift from the book to the necklace and placed her left hand around it. "This is my mother's. You can't have it. These treasures are not here for your benefit. Now be gone," Opaline said.

And before he knew what was going on, he felt himself being pushed back into the human world. "No! No!"

There was nothing he could do. The crack Opaline and Eamon had created by opening the book was closing. Drifting through space, he finally fell and landed.

Groaning, he got to his feet, ready to battle his

daughter and her soulmate, but he wasn't in the book-store. He'd been thrust back to the farmhouse, in the attic.

What the hell? Never in all of his life had anything like this happened to him.

Damn it. He was the Ancient One. Madder than an angry beast, Alyaaluladonati screamed. "One, two, and three will be mine! This will bring about your decline!"

Each word produced a string, and they tied themselves together. With his hands, he pulled the ends tight until there was nothing left of the knot or the string.

When he was satisfied his spell would work, he began to repair the damage his daughter had done. Next time he'd be better prepared to take her on along with her sisters.

thirty-one

Opaline stood clutching the book. The man, her father, had disappeared. Not sure what to do, she was thankful when Eamon clasped her hand.

"No matter what happens, I am here," Opaline stated and squeezed his hand.

"I know. Our love is all we need to protect us."

She smiled. Yes, their love would protect them until the end of time in this universe and on Earth. Looking over her shoulder, she saw her mother had vanished too.

"I have a feeling this isn't going to be the end of Alyaaluladonati. You and I might have wounded him, but he needs this book and the stones that fit into the cover."

"Your mother said that the three of you will defeat the Ancient One. Could Ebba be your half-sister? If she is, who is the third sister?"

Not able to answer his questions, she suggested they go look to see if they could find someone to help them. They wandered the halls of the palace, only to find themselves alone. She felt as if everyone was still around them, but they couldn't see them.

They found a bench that overlooked a valley and sat holding each other. The sky turned orange and blue as the sun rose in the distance. They had made it until morning.

"I think it's time for us to leave," Opaline said.

"I was thinking the same thing. When we get back, pinch me so I know what had happened really did happen. But how do we leave?"

She smiled and put her hand on his cheek. "I love you, Eamon."

"I love you, Opaline, with all my heart." He leaned in and kissed her, sealing their commitment. How she had found the love of her life in a matter of less than a week was a miracle. No, a blessing.

"This place has filled the void of my life. I understand the magic of being a witch. I know what I need to do."

"I trust you. Lead the way."

She stood, and so did Eamon. Taking his hand into hers, she touched the stone in the necklace with her other hand.

"May the world I visited allow me to take my leave. As predicted, as one of three, I believe."

As she chanted the verse she'd created at that moment, things around them began to dissolve. The castle and the beautiful colors vanished. She and Eamon were once again in the sitting room in her bookstore. Ebba was yelling her name. And there was no sign of Alyaaluladonati.

"We're back, Ebba. Everything is okay," Opaline said.

Eamon pulled her into his arms and kissed her again. "Let's not do that again."

"I agree." She was relieved to be home, but a sense of

loss lingered over her. Her mother would never be able to leave the other universe. And once her and her sister's mission was completed, the tear in their two worlds would close.

"Tell me everything. You guys were gone for like minutes," Ebba said.

"Minutes? It was a day for us. The other universe is beautiful. I have no words to describe it. My mother helped us send Alyaaluladonati back here. He is my father. He looks like the drawing of the man we found. We have to keep a lookout for him. My mother also confirmed I have two sisters. You have to be one of them. I'm sure you are. But we'll have to find our other sister. She also told me that if we want to be rid of the Ancient One, Alyaaluladonati, the three of us have to do it."

"Your mother is alive, and we know who our father is? How can that be?"

"My mother is being protected by someone from over there. When she died here, they were able to bring her over there just in time. But she will never be able to leave."

"Opaline, I'm sorry."

Eamon put his arm around her. "It was our love that helped bring us back to Earth. We fought the Ancient One. Opaline's mother said it would take the power of the ONE to truly defeat him."

"She did. But she warned us it had to be done in order. I didn't understand it until now." Opaline pulled out of Eamon's embrace and rushed over to the checkout counter. Grabbing a piece of paper, she began to write names. "According to my mother, there are always three witches. Their names tell the order. So if I put my name first because of the letter O and then my mother's name,

Neveah, for the letter *N*. That leaves Eamon's name for the letter *E*. See they spell ONE."

They stared at her as if she'd lost her mind. Ebba was frowning, but then, as if a light had come on, she rushed over to her side.

"Okay. Let's work on mine. I would go on the bottom for the letter *E*, and my mother, Olexa, would go on top for the letter *O*. Does that mean the love of my life has to have a name that starts with the letter *N*?"

Opaline nodded. "This confirms we have another sister, and her name begins with the letter *N*, and her mother's name started with the letter *O*."

Ebba looked at Opaline. "You better have that next speed dating event soon if I'm going to find my soulmate."

Even after all the sadness and the power-struggle battle they had fought, Opaline understood what it meant to be one.

She slipped her hand into Eamon's and felt his strength. Tomorrow was another day.

May the gods bless the one.

UNTIL WE MET AGAIN.

epilogue

Nevaeh watched her daughter leave the plane that had saved her and her two friends.

"Be strong little one," she said.

"Don't worry. The others will come to her aid."

She looked over her shoulder and saw her friends, Olexa and Eeva, had joined her. The three of them had been brought over when Alyaaluladonati had killed them on their daughters' twenty-first birthday.

"How can I not be worried? He will try everything to kill our daughters too. There have been so many others over the years," Nevaeh sobbed and wiped at her tears.

"Our daughters will prevail. I have seen it. We have to guide them the best we can from here," Olexa stated.

"You both are right. It takes the power of the ONE. We did our best to protect them. They must work together to banish him," Eeva murmured.

"The Gods here are not pleased with him. It's to our daughter's advantage they don't want him here. But we have to be steadfast in our goal," Nevaeh declared and took their hands. "Let's give them more of our blessings to help them."

The other two nodded and together they joined hands, forming a circle and chanted.

"Hush, hush, little ones. Everything will be all right. It's your time to shine. Believe in ONE. By candlelight. Use the stone, the thyme, to make it fine. Trust in ONE."

Don't miss out on your next favorite book!

Join the Satin Romance mailing list
www.satinromance.com/mail.html

THANK YOU FOR READING

Did you enjoy this book?

We invite you to leave a review at your favorite book site, such as Goodreads, Amazon, Barnes & Noble, etc.

DID YOU KNOW THAT LEAVING A REVIEW...

- Helps other readers find books they may enjoy.
- Gives you a chance to let your voice be heard.
- Gives authors recognition for their hard work.
- Doesn't have to be long. A sentence or two about why you liked the book will do.

about the author

I was born and raised in the cold and beautiful Minnesota, but I escaped to Illinois for seventeen years to raise my two boys, and now I call Florida home. My husband Andy, who's always been my hero, has put up with my late night computer typing and endless stacks of papers with my stories on them. We have two furry friends as family; Cookie, an Assui-Po dog and Chip, a ragdoll cat, that their sons compare to Eeyore. They are both getting up there in years now.

Life has been full of ups and downs, but I've made it through the hard times. I love to travel and go to Disney World to trade pins. I've been a bowler for many years, and you can catch me writing my next novel at the lanes.

I encourage you to check out my website for more info and don't be surprised if I let my Norwegian heritage come through in my stories.

Go Vikings! You betcha!

www.sonjagunter.com

also by sonja gunter

WITH SATIN ROMANCE

The Witch's DNA Trilogy

Opaline's Discovery

Nadia's Truth (Coming 2025)

Novels

Waves of Chances

If Yesterday Could Talk

Galloping into Marriage

Love Horsing Around

Holiday Novels

Who's Been Naughty or Nice

Avoiding My Merry Birthday

Anthologies

Apple Pie Delight

in Food & Romance Go Together, Vol. 1